The
Lion's
Share

VIKING
Mystery
Suspense

The Lion's Share

Kelly A. Tate
and
Jack Hanna

VIKING

VIKING
Published by the Penguin Group
Viking Penguin, a division of Penguin Books USA Inc.,
375 Hudson Street, New York, New York 10014, U.S.A.
Penguin Books Ltd, 27 Wrights Lane,
London W8 5TZ, England
Penguin Books Australia Ltd, Ringwood,
Victoria, Australia
Penguin Books Canada Ltd, 10 Alcorn Avenue, Suite 300,
Toronto, Ontario, Canada M4V 3B2
Penguin Books (N.Z.) Ltd, 182–190 Wairau Road,
Auckland 10, New Zealand

Penguin Books Ltd, Registered Offices:
Harmondsworth, Middlesex, England

First published in 1992 by Viking Penguin,
a division of Penguin Books USA Inc.

1 3 5 7 9 10 8 6 4 2

PUBLISHER'S NOTE
This is a work of fiction. Names, characters, places, and incidents
either are the product of the author's imagination or are used
fictitiously, and any resemblance to actual persons, living or
dead, events, or locales is entirely coincidental.

LIBRARY OF CONGRESS CATALOGING IN PUBLICATION DATA
Tate, Kelly Anne.
The lion's share / Kelly A. Tate with Jack Hanna.
p.   cm.
ISBN 0–670–84011–4
I. Hanna, Jack, 1947– . II. Title.
PS3570.A825L5   1992
813'.54—dc20   91-37483

Printed in the United States of America
Set in Times Roman

For
Kaitlee and Cameran

A prince, being thus obliged to know well how to act as a beast, must imitate the fox and the lion, for the lion cannot protect himself from traps, and the fox cannot defend himself from wolves. One must therefore be a fox to recognize traps, and a lion to frighten wolves.

—Niccolò Machiavelli (1469–1527),
The Prince (1532), Chapter 17

The Lion's Share

Chapter 1

"Don't move, Doc."

The voice was low and came from somewhere just behind veterinarian Carlson "Mac" MacIntire. He barely caught a glimpse of Nat Watermann out of the corner of his eye as the zookeeper inched his way past him. Mac lay prostrate on the cold cement floor, the 300-pound lioness draped across him in a full-body press. He smiled wryly. He could hardly breathe, much less move. Pinned, he nodded a slow, cautious fraction of an inch.

Mac stifled a groan as needle-sharp claws dug through the flimsy material of his shirt into bare flesh. His right arm was free but each time he moved, the lioness tightened her grip, her mouth clamping around his neck to immobilize her prey. Her tail twitched rhythmically from side to side as she straddled his body, her stubby fur like prickly nettle. Two-inch glistening white teeth flashed just above him as Sheba snarled at Watermann's movement.

Mac could see the handle of the tranquilizer gun lying overhead on the treatment table. He had been reaching for it just as she came at him. Now one wrong move, one careless gesture and the young lioness, only acting her part of the mighty hunter, would attack in earnest.

She began to lick his neck at the hairline, attracted by the sweat that ran in small channels down his face. The raspy tongue felt like industrial-gauge sandpaper, slowly grating away the sensitive skin. Her hot breath smelled heavily of raw meat and old blood.

"Doc, she's not gonna let me get to the tranq," said Watermann. "I'm going for the hose."

Minutes stretched. Mac shut his eyes. The young animal relaxed, growled softly, her front paws kneading painfully into the vet's ribs. He flinched involuntarily. Sheba tightened her hold, one canine tooth puncturing through skin. Mac tried not to think of what could happen—and had happened to more than one zookeeper. They had resembled golf balls, pocked bodies of consumed flesh, before help could arrive.

The water hit him with a force that took his breath away. Watermann had returned with William Decker, another zookeeper, who trained the fire hose on the animal's massive head and chest. Indignant, she lunged her six-foot length at the source of the water, a huge paw slicing an empty instant of space in the deluge. Her snarls muffled by the roar of the water, she battled the torrent that drove her relentlessly backward.

Mac rolled quickly away, in the direction of the treatment table. Reaching up he snatched the tranquilizer gun and aimed, waiting to see if it was necessary to fire. Watermann had moved to just beside the exam-room door and calmly held a .45 revolver. He looked fully prepared to stop her.

Sheba retreated into the far corner. From there Decker herded the cat into her enclosure with short bursts of water. The sound of the 200-pound iron door hitting cement reverberated through the small room.

Mac raked back a mass of dark hair plastered to his forehead and glanced ruefully at the remnants of his favorite shirt, now hanging in shredded disarray. Two puncture sites oozed blood from just above the left nipple.

"You okay?" asked Watermann, swinging him to his feet.

Water ran down Mac in streams onto the floor. "I think I just got religion."

Watermann grinned. "That'll do it," he said, clapping the big man on the shoulder. After only two weeks at the Rockland Zoo, the keepers already liked the new vet. Doc MacIntire played it straight. A welcomed change after all that had been going on lately.

Mac sloshed into his office and began peeling off wet clothing. A voice from the doorway made him turn as he tentatively dabbed hydrogen peroxide on the chest wounds.

"Lions, huh? Figured you for a little kinky," said Donald Stewart. The general manager was a little man who, by either bad luck or bad genes, was completely bald and only thirty.

"Just a new form of primal therapy I was trying out," Mac said.

"Did it work?"

"Too early to tell."

Stewart laughed, his fifth shirt button barely restraining a jiggling mid-torso bulge. Although he didn't look like the management type, Donald Stewart was organized, dedicated, and totally supportive of his staff. It was nice to finally be able to relax and just do the job, Mac thought. No more tiptoeing through politics and departmental infighting.

Of course, the Massachusetts zoo was not as prestigious a facility as the one he had just left, but he planned to change all that. Ten years of intensive work in zoo medicine had given him the clout to head his own program. And, more importantly, Stewart was going to let him do it. At least Stewart's ego was in good shape.

It was only a month ago he had seen the Rockland Zoo's advertisement for a veterinarian with experience in carnivore reproduction for its Red Wolf Species Survival Plan. Mac had flown out the next morning. Donald Stewart, who had been single-handedly running the endangered-wolf program, had met him at the Delta baggage claim. The two men hit it off immediately. After a brief interview with H. L. Hargreve, the zoo's director, Mac knew this was where he wanted to be.

The jungles of Vietnam had been an in-depth lesson on the fragility of life—human or otherwise. There Mac had vowed, one particularly savage night, to try to give back something to the human condition after having taken so much from it. Too many years later, Rockland and the red wolves were just what he needed to finally honor that promise. To try to save a little part of creation. Mac had packed and headed east.

•   •   •

The zebra-striped golf cart coasted to a stop beside the main building. Joanne Nordstrom, the receptionist, looked up from a press release about an impending gorilla birth as Mac and Stewart entered the office. In her late twenties, Joanne looked out of place at the metal business desk. She should have been following a path through untouched wilderness somewhere. A natural in hiking boots and a backpack.

"Hey, Doc, how's Molly doing today? Any sign?"

Mac shook his head. The gorilla was frustratingly overdue.

"So, how do you like the job?" she asked. "And our new director . . . ?" Her voice seemed to crack slightly.

"Job's great. But I should have held out for a car like Hargreve's," Mac replied. He had spotted the new director's flashy Mercedes 560SL disappearing around the rear of the executive building early that morning. Decker entered the office just in time to agree.

"Course I'd settle for the Hargreve ring," Stewart added.

Joanne's head jerked up. "Ring? But H. L.'s . . ." She

stopped mid-sentence. She had turned pale underneath her tan.

"You okay?" Decker asked.

Joanne smiled broadly at the keeper. "I just hate it when a man's diamond is bigger than mine."

Mac glanced down. Joanne wasn't wearing jewelry.

From his belt Stewart's walkie-talkie squawked a summons from the new director. "Speak of the devil," he muttered.

After his interview with H. L. Hargreve, Mac hadn't spoken with anyone at the Massachusetts zoo before he left California on his drive east. But upon arriving in Boston a month later, Mac found the zoo reeling from Hargreve's tragic death while on safari in Africa. A new director, Edward Hargreve, H. L.'s son, had already been appointed by the zoo's Board of Directors.

Mac and Stewart stepped out of the front office into the late-morning sunlight. Climbing into the golf cart, they threaded their way slowly through a stream of visitors. For a weekday, the zoo was crowded. Families wandered down the crisscrossing paths that ran alongside the animals' naturalistic enclosures. A small group of noisy schoolchildren was being herded along by a battalion of harried teachers. Mac grinned at one five-year-old who was dawdling along. The little boy was about the same age as his son. Or would have been. Mac pushed the thought away. Just inside her wire-mesh barricade a slender cheetah followed stealthily behind the two men, her coat rippling from good health.

Mac had been impressed by the zoo, located fifteen miles southeast of Boston. Each species' winter shelter was surrounded by grounds that closely resembled its natural homeland. Wide moats kept the animals from escaping, yet allowed ample movement and cover. In some of the larger areas, predator and prey lived within feet of each other, separated by cleverly hidden fences, piano wire, and plexiglass screens. Mac could see the lioness Sheba, his morning's dance partner, lounging regally on a bluff overlooking a herd of impala. She looked none the worse for wear.

H. L. Hargreve had turned the once-shabby New England zoo into a facility with an international reputation for progressive reproduction techniques. His unending energy and millions from his personal fortune had been the primary catalysts.

Mac turned to the general manager. "What exactly happened to H. L., anyway? I heard, poachers. They get 'em?"

Stewart stopped the cart abruptly in front of the pachyderm exhibit and leaned his forearms on the steering wheel. He stared out at an African bull elephant, Koko, rolling a huge log stump around with his trunk as if it were a twig.

"Nope. H. L. went to Kenya to finish off his work on their new national game preserve. He'd been helping them for two years. Was about done." Stewart swatted at an insect circling his left ear. "He and Decker, one of our zookeepers who has worked in Africa as a guide—and about eight Kenyans—had camped out in an area that had been having problems with ivory poaching. H. L. wanted to see for himself. He was like that. They'd waited there a few days and were getting low on supplies, so he sent Decker to a town twenty miles away. Decker got back at dusk and found the whole party wiped. Automatic weapons. Real well equipped. Blew them away."

Mac whistled softly through his teeth.

"Really shook this place up. Decker'd been on staff only a couple of months and he had to bring H. L.'s body back. That'd be tough for anybody." Stewart paused. "Then the fighting started about who'd be the next director. Suddenly Ed Hargreve stepped up and volunteered. Edward is H. L.'s son." Stewart leaned out of the cart, started to spit, caught himself, and swallowed.

"Knew they were related," said Mac.

"By blood only." Stewart scowled off at some distant point.

"Board acted like he was the damn Second Coming. . . ." Stewart straightened, checked his watch, and abruptly accelerated off toward the director's building, a set look to his lower jaw.

The foyer was like stepping into another world. A life-size mural of exotic plants and animals was painted on three walls. The fourth wall was floor-to-ceiling glass with a cascade of plants and flowers. A toco toucan's gigantic yellow beak bobbed in the dark-green foliage. Just above a small cascading brook, an electric-blue hyacinthine macaw stood one-legged, munching casually on a Brazil nut. Mac half expected to hear drumbeats. The two men took the stairs up to the second floor and entered the Executive Suite.

Claire Burke sat on the secretary's chair behind her mahogany L-shaped desk. Mac could see long stockinged legs disappearing underneath the desk's massive top as she added a layer of coral lipstick to her lips. Claire was the rare kind of woman who, while not drop-dead gorgeous, was unexpectedly stunning. Mac unconsciously smoothed down the front of his shirt.

"Want me to blot that for you?"

"In your dreams, Stewart," Claire said and laughed. She put down the mirror, her eyes moving to Mac as he leaned against the doorjamb. She ran her fingers through her shoulder-length brown hair.

"Mr. Hargreve is waiting to see you. I'll let him know you're here." She smiled warmly at Mac, who tried not to gawk as she disappeared into the director's office. He turned to find Stewart watching him, a grin on his face.

"Don't say one word," Mac said. Claire appeared in the doorway and they followed her gesture into the director's office.

Ed Hargreve fussed with a gold cuff link at the edge of his custom shirtsleeve as he sat behind a desk twice as large as was necessary. Mac settled down in one of the burgundy leather high-back chairs positioned opposite the director.

This was the first good look Mac had gotten at his new boss. For some reason he had assumed Edward would sport the same no-nonsense attitude as the senior Hargreve. But Oriental rugs and strategically placed objets d'art had appeared in place of steel and broadloom. Mac squirmed uncomfortably, noticing a piece of dried manure stuck to the heel of his work boot.

The originator of the new decor was finishing a telephone conversation as the two men waited. A huge diamond flashed from the third finger of Hargreve's phone hand. Even Mac, who didn't take much interest in gems, could appraise the rock from across the room. Minutes stretched on. Stewart stared at the ceiling, tunelessly whistling under his breath.

Mac stared half seeing out of the office's picture window. The zoo's 280 landscaped acres stretched in all directions, grouping their 4000 animals into geographical areas. Mac was vaguely aware of a khaki-uniformed guide busily educating a smallish cluster of what would eventually total a half-million annual visitors.

The Rockland Zoo was prosperous in comparison to many. And under H. L. Hargreve's leadership, it had led the cause for endangered species, making a major impact on current attitudes about the environment and the planet. Rockland was a big business, dressed up, all fuzzy and furry, Mac thought.

"Dr. MacIntire," Hargreve said as he hung up the phone. "Glad to have you aboard." He offered the diamond-clad hand.

"Mac . . . call me Mac." The hand felt like a research rat on heavy downers. Mac restrained the urge to wipe his own on his pants leg.

"Yes, well, Dr. MacIntire, I read your proposal for the red-wolf project. Of course I will handle getting the breeding plan approved by the species survival propagation committee."

Mac shifted in his chair, feeling more uncomfortable by the second. Coordinating Rockland's plan with the national zoo association was a part of his job. Out of the corner of his eye

Mac could see Stewart inspecting the rug's design as his jaw muscles clenched and unclenched.

H. L. Hargreve had conducted Mac's job interview while shoveling out a giraffe stall. His son didn't look like a man who made his own bed.

"Tell me, Doctor—" the custom pin-striped suit leaned back, fingers folded neatly across the tailored vest—"have you given any thought—"

"Mr. Hargreve, Mr. Locke is on the phone." Claire's voice boomed over the intercom. Hargreve took the call from Hilton Locke, chairman of the zoo's Board of Directors.

"Yes, Hilt . . . talk to Cristos . . . he's in charge of the audit . . . I just spend it, right?" The director laughed a shade too loudly.

Mac hadn't met the new chief financial officer, Alex Cristos, but rumor had it he was a tough, bottom-line type. Mac had run into this business-school-grad mentality before. It made getting certain expensive medical supplies difficult. But zoos were facing reduced funding and increased overhead, and were having to merge, somewhat uncomfortably, with the business world in order to survive. The whole concept grated Mac the wrong way.

As Hargreve hung up, the intercom crackled again. "You have a luncheon date with the mayor in ten minutes at the Espadrille, Mr. Hargreve." Claire's voice sounded starched and formal.

The suit unfolded without a wrinkle as the director stood to show the men out. "We'll have to continue this later, gentlemen."

Hargreve extended his hand as they stood at his private doorway to the hall. From behind them sneakers squeaked loudly on the floor's linoleum, as a tall, gangly man in his early twenties shuffled past. The zoo's navy-blue security uniform hung on him like a Hefty trash bag.

"Just a minute there," Hargreve said to the guard. "What are those?" Mac could hear the sarcasm practically dripping onto the floor. He didn't know the kid, but he felt bad for him already.

The guard's acne-pocked face flushed an unnatural scarlet. "Ah . . . sneakers, sir," he stammered.

"What is your name?"

"Vincent. Jeff Vincent," he mumbled into his chest. Mac and Stewart looked at each other. Hargreve was clearly enjoying this.

"Get the regulation boots or don't come to work. Understand?"

Vincent nodded and hurried off. Mac glanced down at his own boot, hesitated, and deliberately scuffed the piece of feces off onto the director's Persian carpet.

"By the way, Edward, when can I expect the funds for the aviary project? The Building Committee has approved the final plans and the architect will have the blueprints by the end of the week," Stewart asked.

Hargreve adjusted his other cuff link. "Sorry, there's been a change. The avian project has been put on hold. We'll get to it as soon as we can, of course."

Stewart's neck muscles began to define themselves like a cobra in a warning stance. "But that project has been in the works for over a year." He seemed to be breathing harder.

"Sorry, we just can't fund it at the moment."

"Wait one minute, Edward. A million dollars was set aside by the Board months ago. We were just waiting for the plans."

Mac shifted from one foot to the other. As he glanced back into the office, his eyes met Claire's. She shrugged and went back to the papers in front of her.

"Stewart, as the new director, I had to make some hard decisions as to how to run this zoo. The Board agreed with my recommendation to put it on hold."

Stewart's eyes fixed on the director's Adam's apple as if he wanted to personally measure the custom shirt's neck size. He took a half step forward as Hargreve pivoted on his heel and walked back into his office. The heavy door shut with a firm click.

Mac decided it was a good time to remember a monkey that needed checking and excused himself. At this new job he was determined not to get dragged into the politics.

He had thought, once upon a time, that being part of management was the way to change things. He had found it an exercise in abject frustration. He liked, no needed, the hands-on care of the animals. Somehow they gave him a sense of balance. Something to counteract the world's day-after-day grinding defeats—a species lost here, a rain forest there.

As soon as he had arrived in Rockland he had started a policy of twenty-four-hour video monitoring of all sick, pregnant, and postoperative animals. The docents, an energetic volunteer staff of town residents, had eagerly agreed to provide the 5:00 P.M. to 7:00 A.M. watch. Here, at least, he could reduce the losses. Rockland was his baby now.

Mac took his time walking to the video monitoring department. He immediately noticed some additions to the tiny monitoring room. A new coffee machine stood on top of a small refrigerator humming away in one corner. Three monitors stared blankly, waiting for their nightly vigil. Mac opened the order book and jotted down today's instructions for Sienna, an injured female red wolf.

Esther, the docent director, stuck her head around the corner as Mac scribbled orders. "Another monitor? Who?"

"Sienna. I just moved her into the confinement pen next to the main wolf enclosure. She'll pace herself on that bad leg and I want to know what that pacing is. I'll come review the tape each morning."

It had taken seven pins and six hours of surgery to save

Sienna's leg. According to Stewart, who had practically hand-raised the entire thirteen-member pack, Sienna had always been the lowest-ranking female. Meke, the dominant female, had chewed her up badly over some territorial dispute.

In the wild, Meke would have driven her out of the pack, to struggle, maybe even die, on her own. But now, with only 160 remaining red wolves in the world, each animal was priceless. Stewart and a team of docents had stayed with her around the clock for two weeks while she was most critical. Like many things at the zoo, it had been a labor of love.

Rockland's red wolves were prospering now, due in large part to Stewart's devotion. They were the manager's children, each lovingly cared for, and in return they allowed the little man to join them inside the habitat, as a part of their family group.

Mac left the orders for Esther and walked to his office just off the main corridor of the big cat compound. The office was small compared to his last one, but a south-facing window let in the September sun, making it cozy. He propped his oversized work boots on top of a desk that looked older than he was. The office's furniture reminded him of an old World War II movie. Betty Grable could have sauntered in at any moment.

He turned to the shortest of many looming piles of paperwork randomly stacked about the office. He hated all the record keeping that zoo animals required, but had resigned himself to it long ago. Mac let out a sigh and opened the first manila folder, labeled "Ivory," a white tiger with a pad laceration.

A fly buzzed softly from somewhere near the windowpane. The office became warm as the early-afternoon sun migrated slowly across the dusty floor. Mac's chin began to inch down onto the front of the khaki shirt. He fought it briefly, the easy slide of sleep, then went with it.

This was one of the nice ones, this dream. It always started the same way, with Sara laughing, kicking the white foam of a wave, as they walk along. The warm sun lies heavy on his skin. He can feel the sand under his bare toes, the wedding ring digging gently into his third finger as she curls her fingers between his. She says something he can't catch in that little-girl way she has. . . .

The walkie-talkie seemed to jump in its spot on the desk as a voice filled with urgency burst from the small speaker, shattering the dream. Unconsciously, he reached for Sara, trying to hold her, to keep her.

"Signal One, Snake, Front Office. Unit Eighty-one to Unit Ninety-four, Unit Eighty-one to Unit Ninety-four. Come in."

Mac recognized the emergency code. Grabbing the phone, he dialed the front-desk number. Stewart answered on the first ring.

"Mac, get here fast. Joanne Nordstrom was bitten about fifteen minutes ago by what the keepers think is a mamba. She's having trouble breathing."

"Jesus Christ, a mamba! Where the hell . . . tell her to lie down, don't move around. Call an ambulance. I'll be right there."

Mac leapt from the chair, running into the adjoining exam room and surgical suite. In the far corner, padlocked, was a small refrigerator used exclusively for antivenin. Mac's hands trembled slightly as he searched for the color-coded key on the huge key ring he carried. The door opened on the first try. Mac sorted through the cluttered collection of ten-milliliter vials of the venom antidote. He silently vowed to organize them as he found the five vials of white crystalline powder, started to turn, and realized something was wrong. The vials should have been ice cold.

Changes in temperature, and especially heat, deactivate snake antivenin, making it as useless as tap water. Cold fear began to move up his chest as he felt the warm glass bottles. The refrigerator sat lifeless. He had checked the machine just yesterday, in fact, three days before the required weekly inspection. Mac always played it safe.

He pocketed the ampules and ran to the far wall, tearing open the glass doors of the treatment cabinet. Grabbing handfuls of syringes, alcohol swabs, and cotton two-by-twos, he stuffed them into his black treatment bag. Racing from the office, he dodged visitors like a broken-field runner.

The vet burst through the front office's door just as a six-foot snake arched three feet of its body into the air, mouth open, flashing its deathly black interior. The mamba spread its neck wide, shook its head, and hissed, threatening two reptile keepers who slowly circled with snares. One yelled, without turning, "She's in the side office. It's a mamba. Been 'bout fifteen—maybe twenty—minutes since the strike."

Mac quietly opened the office door. Joanne lay stretched out on the carpet, her mouth a pale-blue ring. He could hear her breathing from where he stood. Sweat beaded and ran down off her face onto the rug. Fear reached up into his throat. Stewart was leaning over the woman, talking to her softly. He looked up as the vet entered, relief on his face.

"Joanne, it's going to be okay, Mac's here with the antivenin."

Mac motioned Stewart over to him. "Get on the phone, find the closest facility with West African polyvalent and get it airlifted to the nearest hospital. And get that ambulance here fast!" he whispered urgently. "Ours may not be any good." He started pulling out the syringes.

"You're not going to give that to her here! She could have a reaction. . . . It could kill her!"

"We can't wait. Look at her, she's going into respiratory collapse."

Horror crept across Stewart's face as he turned, glanced back at the woman, and then hurried from the room. Mac knelt beside Joanne. He could easily count the rapid rise and fall of the woman's chest. Placing a finger on the side of her throat, he felt the woman's pulse hammering away at three times the normal rate. Terror flashed from Joanne's blue eyes. Sara had had that same look, he thought. Mac forced away the paralysis that seemed to be spreading through his arms. "Take it easy, Joanne, everything will be fine," he lied.

Mac quickly wiped off the vials' rubber stoppers with the alcohol swabs. Drawing back on a syringe, he inserted it into a bottle of sterile water, then injected the liquid into the first bottle of white antivenin powder, and shook it. The drug rapidly turned fluid. He withdrew the antidote into the syringe, wiped down Joanne's arm, and inserted the needle into her vein.

As little as two drops of a mamba's neurotoxic venom can kill an adult. He gave Joanne all five vials, small dots of blood welling up at each injection site.

Mac glanced down. On her leg, about mid-thigh, were two puncture holes encircled by bright red, swollen skin. He wrapped a tight band around her leg just above the bite, hoping to slow the upward spread of venom. Suctioning a bite from this kind of snake was futile. Everything, her life, was riding on the effects of the antitoxin. Warm antitoxin.

Joanne was trying to speak, her voice hoarse and strangled. The sound of vocal cord paralysis saturated the small office. Where the hell was that ambulance? The woman needed oxygen and treatment for shock.

Joanne reached up and grabbed him by the shirt, pulling him down close. "Ring . . ." Mac looked at her, confused. "H. L. . . . Listen to me. . . . The . . ." She seemed to be panicking.

"Relax, Joanne, you can tell me later at the hospital." He stroked her hair, trying to calm her and himself. "It's okay, you'll be fine."

Stewart hurried into the office with the EMT crew right behind. Joanne was showing no sign of improvement. Mac pulled one of the ambulance crew aside. "She's got a pulse of one hundred eighty, respirations are fifty-two and shallow, and she's beginning to show signs of dyspnea. In the last few minutes she's had increasing circumoral cyanosis. I gave her fifty milliliters of antivenin intravenously five minutes ago. But she's not responding—it may not be any good."

The ambulance driver looked at him closely. "Thanks, you a doctor or something?"

"I'm the new vet here—but used to be a medic."

The EMTs quickly started an IV, put the young woman on the stretcher, and rushed her from the office, a green oxygen mask obscuring her struggle to breathe. Mac leaned against the wall, fighting the old panic.

Stewart peered at him. Turning from the manager's scrutiny, Mac snapped the needle hub from the syringe barrel. It almost slipped from his shaking fingers.

"They get the snake?" Mac managed to ask as he walked shakily into the outer office. The reptile keepers were just finishing crating the angry, writhing mamba.

Mac had never seen one close up. Most zoos considered them too ill tempered, too dangerous to keep. As he approached the clear container, the snake bent back laterally, displayed its prominent fangs, and struck at him. Whitish venom ran slowly down the crate's side in small rivulets.

At only an hour of age, a young mamba can already kill a rat in a blinding series of bites. The snakes had more than earned their feared reputation as one of the few snakes in the world that will attack a man. Mambas were even known to strike windshields of passing trucks in their African homeland. Mac could well believe all of it as the large, prominent black eyes glared at him with unconcealed hatred. He involuntarily took a step backward.

One of the snake keepers was securing the cover on the crate of the second snake, a harmless green tree snake. The two reptiles looked disquietingly similar.

"What the hell happened, Jack?" Mac asked the keeper.

"Don't really know. Got a page from Joanne that someone had just donated two tree snakes. She picked up the box to move it off the front desk and the bottom gave way. She said the snakes were loose in the office and asked us to come get them. . . . We didn't hurry 'cause, a tree snake's not like, well, a big deal." The keeper nervously ran a hand through his hair. "Anyway, we got here and found the tree snake halfway up that ficus tree over there. So, we started teasing Joanne that next she would be calling us 'bout bats in her belfry. Then she tells us one bit her. . . . Honest, Doc, that was the first time we heard 'bout any bite. She started acting kinda funny, all sweaty and stuff. Thought maybe she was kiddin' us, so I went over and was lookin' at her leg, when I heard 'Holy shit' from Frank. Damn if that snake wasn't sitting up just like my damn beagle, coming right at him."

Frank, the other reptile keeper, joined the two men. "Took me back a couple, I'll tell ya," Frank said. "Never run into a mamba, loose, like that. Man, they're fast."

"That's when I knew Jo was in big trouble. I paged you and Stewart an' went after that sucker. Fastest snake I've ever seen—and ain't even a year old. Sure wouldn't want to tangle with an adult."

"I thought mambas were black; that one's green," Mac said.

"Once they're grown. Some are green when young—sorta olive. That's what first tipped me off it wasn't no tree snake, when I saw his ass sticking out from under the desk," Frank said.

The keepers were gingerly gathering up the snake crates when Decker and Watermann rushed into the front office.

"What can we do?" Decker asked, taking off his jacket and starting to roll up his sleeves.

"Thanks, but we got 'em handled," Frank replied. The

keeper balanced the crate at arm's length. Watermann held the door open for them.

"I hate those things," Decker confided to Mac. "Snakes are about the only thing that make me real nervous. Ran into mambas a lot in Africa. Nasty bastards."

Mac had to agree. Hot-tempered lethal snakes weren't his favorites either. It took a special type to work with them. But at six-foot-two and every ounce of 240 pounds, Decker didn't look like he'd be afraid of much of anything.

Fifteen minutes later Stewart walked back into the office. "All set?"

Stewart nodded, slowly.

"Where's the antivenin coming from?"

"New York. It's already in the air."

Mac looked at his watch. The men looked at each other and then away. Mac angrily punched the cardboard box that had contained the snakes. It fell off the desk and did a slow roll onto its lid, the once-taped bottom gaping open. Mac bent over to pick it up and noticed a series of thin marks running across the bottom's masking tape. The tape looked scored, deliberately weakened.

Mac carefully ran his finger back and forth across the tape. He was about to say something when Stewart read the release form the snake donator had signed. "Ralph Danesto. Lives in Malden. What kind of idiot would have a black mamba in Boston?"

"Probably kept it in his basement," Mac said. "Some snake hobbyists are pretty crazy. I know one that sleeps with an adult rattlesnake in a fish tank at the head of his bed."

"Would kind of discourage any overnight guests, wouldn't it?" Stewart said, forcing a grin.

The front-office telephone rang. Stewart picked up the phone. There was a long silence as he listened to someone on the other end. He said good-bye softly and eased the receiver back on the cradle. Without turning, he said, "The antivenin just arrived. . . . She . . . Joanne didn't make it."

Mac slammed out of the office door into the bright afternoon, a small group of Japanese tourists leaping out of his way. He stormed into his office and strode to the treatment room. Pulling the ring of keys out of his pocket, he unlocked the refrigerator door. The collection of little antivenin vials sat as he had left them, warm and useless.

The power switch indicated that the refrigerator was on. He grabbed hold of the machine and yanked it away from the wall. The plug sat securely in place in the outlet socket. Then he noticed the pool of condensation on the floor. He felt the machine's cooling coils, still and lifeless. His fist hitting the top of the cabinet sent a spray of ampules rattling across the floor.

● ● ●

Robert Kirby parked his unmarked police car right in front of the zoo's entrance, blocking the handicap ramp. The black-and-whites were already there. The call had come in in the middle of a chopped-chicken-liver-and-onion sandwich. He popped a Tums into his mouth and was still chewing it as he entered the zoo's front office.

"Everyone here?" he asked the uniformed policewoman in position at the door.

"Yes, sir, three keepers from the surrounding exhibits, the general manager, the veterinarian, and the two snake keepers. The director's secretary, Claire Burke, is here to show you to his office. He'll see you whenever you're ready."

"I'm ready. This'll be cut-and-dried. Some nosy broad stuck it where it didn't belong and now she's dead."

The policewoman gave him an icy look.

Mac watched the detective walk out in front of the small group, stop, and let the silence lengthen. Kirby looked carefully at each person in the room. The men stared unwaveringly back at him. In the corner sat Claire, crying softly, a soggy tissue balled into one fist.

"Anybody see the guy who donated the snakes—what's his name?" Stewart stood and handed the detective the zoo's donor release form. Kirby scanned it quickly. "Danesto. Ralph Danesto?" He stared expectantly around the room. No one spoke. Claire sniffed audibly. "Okay, we'll get in contact with this guy and find out what other slime he owns.

"Now, who else was in the office when, ah, Joelle Nordstrom was bitten?"

"Joanne, Detective Kirby, Joanne Nordstrom," Stewart said. "She was manning the office by herself during break."

The middle-aged policeman made a few notes. "Alone, huh? Probably got bored and decided to take a peek," he muttered to himself. Kirby looked up. No one was smiling.

Mac stood up. "Detective, I'm Dr. MacIntire, the vet here. Miss Nordstrom told the reptile keepers she had been moving the box off the front desk to a safer location when the bottom fell out. You might want to take a look at it." Mac gestured toward the box.

Kirby walked over and briefly inspected the box. "That's it?"

"That's the story."

"Yeah, uh, thanks," Kirby said. "We'll need a statement from the first few people on the scene. The rest of you give your name to the police officer by the door, then you can go. But I may need to ask you a few questions later."

The detective turned and walked back to the policewoman. "I'll be done here in about fifteen minutes. This case's pretty straightforward." He sighed. "I love 'em when they're neat." He glanced back at MacIntire. "You know that guy? The vet?"

She looked at Mac, who was talking privately with Stewart. "No, why?"

"Don't know. Like I've seen him before."

"Not in Rockland. *That* one I'd remember."

Kirby, irritated, snapped his worn leather notebook shut. "Probably from that research-animal protest last month. This place's nothing but a flaming bunch of bleeding-heart do-good-ers anyway."

The detective waved the reptile keepers into the inner office and was following them in when he heard a soft sob. Claire sat hunched in her chair, tearful, small in her grief. Kirby hesitated, pulled a handkerchief out of his pocket, stared at it, took two steps toward her, dropped it into her lap, and hurried after the keepers.

As Stewart left, Mac turned and watched Kirby through the office door. The detective stood and listened to the snake keep-ers, expressionless, offhandedly scribbling notes. Mac ran his broad hand down over his face and followed the rest of the staff out of the building. He had dealt with this kind of cop before. After a few years on the force they figure they've got everyone pegged. Mac felt old anger rumbling around just above belt level.

Chapter 2

As Edward Hargreve paced past his oversized desk he felt the room getting smaller and more confining by the minute. He was reaching for the phone again when he noticed the man standing in the doorway.

Alex Cristos always seemed to just appear. Every move was slick and quiet. Hargreve jumped despite himself. "Jesus, can't you wear a bell or something. You're like a damn cat." Hargreve straightened his silk tie and sat down behind the desk. The chief financial officer formed his thin smile.

"Lookin' a little twitchy there, Hargreve. You want'd to see me?"

The director held up a sheet of white note paper. The edge trembled slightly. "This—shut the door—I got back from that Nordstrom mess, and *this* was on my desk." He handed it to Cristos.

Across the paper, in bold black ink, someone had scrawled, "This wasn't an accident. I know what you are up to."

Cristos looked up in alarm. It was the first time Hargreve had ever seen him miss a beat.

Alex Cristos set the note down on the desk with deliberate control. His face had gone blank, the perfect poker face. Only a slight bead of perspiration just below the hairline gave him away. He casually lit a thin foreign cigarette. "Where did you find this?"

"On my desk—stuck in the blotter. Claire and I were in the front office. Came back and found it," Hargreve said, standing and stuffing his hands into his trouser pockets. Taking a few nervous paces, he stopped and forced himself to sit down on the edge of the desk. "Couldn't have been gone twenty minutes. Who? . . . Who do you think left this?"

Hargreve stared at the note, dazed. Like magic, Cristos was again back in control. It made Hargreve feel even more flustered and he resented it. "God, somebody knows. . . ."

"It was a fluke. We don't know what this note means. Anyway, the police say Joanne's death was just what it was, an accident. An unfortunate mishap. Relax, you're getting hysterical." Cristos stood up, stubbed the cigarette out in the malachite ashtray, and headed for the door. "Just sit tight. Let him play his next hand. If there is one."

Cristos seemed to vanish from the doorway, one minute there, the next gone. Hargreve hated the way he did that.

•   •   •

Mac had a headache that wouldn't quit. He sat in the front office answering the phones where Joanne had been just hours ago. He couldn't wait until this day was over. The zoo closed in fifteen minutes, then he had to meet a medical consultant, attend one committee meeting, and then he could go home. He'd have a beer. Maybe more than just one.

Mac locked the door to the front office. The Indian summer sun was beginning to dip down behind the top of the gorillas' large play yard. On his left the light reflected off the pleated waves in the small lake next to the zoo's main entrance. Mandarin ducks glided colorfully past a group of parents trying to corral their children.

Cutting across to a path that led to the ape enclosure, Mac could see Molly, the pregnant gorilla, stretched out in maternal plumpness on one of the rope hammocks. The entire town was waiting for her delivery. Gorilla births were a major news item, and attendance would double after the blessed event. Bongo, her mate, beat a rapid tattoo on his chest as another, younger male infringed upon the silverback's favorite tree stump.

Dr. Greenspan, an obstetrician, stood waiting for Mac alongside the enclosure, watching Molly carefully through four-power field glasses. For the primates, physicians were almost as much a part of their medical care as were veterinarians. Human and ape medicine were not all that different; even the drugs used were the same. Darwin would have loved it, Mac thought.

A few remaining visitors straggled toward the exit. The night security guard would be starting his first rounds to make sure all unauthorized persons were off the grounds and the gates locked until the next morning, at 9:00 A.M. Mac glanced toward the guard station in time to see Jeff Vincent, his white sneakers brilliant in the afternoon light, coming out of the building. Mac shook hands with Dr. Greenspan and checked his watch. He had a half hour before the committee meeting started. He and the physician got down to business.

•   •   •

Most of the Executive Committee members were already seated at the conference table. A few stood clustered to the side, talking in low tones. One looked up as Mac entered— Stewart—and waved a greeting from the opposite end of the room.

"You must be Dr. MacIntire?"

Mac turned toward the smooth voice to find an impeccably dressed man standing next to him, smoking a pencil-thin cigarette.

"I'm Alex Cristos, the chief financial officer. Welcome to Rockland. If there's anything I can do to help your start-up here, just let me know." The man's mouth formed a cool, saccharine smile that didn't impact the rest of his face.

Mac shook the equally cool hand. "I'll remember that. So far, Donald Stewart is doing a great job of leading me around."

Cristos made a noncommittal noise and seemed to glide to his chair beside Ed Hargreve. Mac took a seat in the middle of the table and looked around.

The boardroom showed the influence of the new leadership. Rose-colored wall-to-wall carpeting squished thickly underfoot. A twenty-foot conference table put all the members in a football-shaped arrangement. Two oversized abstract oil paintings hung on the wall, softly back lit by museum-style lights. The room would have done justice to any Fortune 500 company. Here where the zoo struggled to preserve endangered, dying species, it rankled.

Hilton Locke, the Board's committee chairman, cleared his throat to indicate the start of the meeting. Mac glanced around at the other members. Hargreve sat between Locke and Cristos. Stewart was at the far end of the table, with an assortment of other unfamiliar men making up the rest of the seventeen-member committee. Claire, sitting slightly behind Hargreve, began to read the minutes of the last meeting. As she did, Hilton Locke shuffled through a large sheaf of yellow legal papers, making notes in the margins as he went along.

Locke looked like a basic, hard-working stiff. Certainly not the type to swing the top executive position at the town's First Security Bank. As he watched him, Mac couldn't picture Locke as a heavy hitter in the Rockland financial sphere. That position was supercharged politics. His appointment as chairman of the zoo's Board, typically an honorary position of no financial value, might have helped get him membership in the country club, but not a position as CEO of the biggest bank in town.

Even in as small a place as Rockland. Okay, so maybe Locke just does a great job and I'm just getting old and cynical, Mac said to himself. He forced his attention back to the meeting.

Claire finished reading the minutes and looked up. Directly into his eyes. Mac found himself staring into dark pupils that melted into rich, warm brown. He pried his eyes away and over to Alex Cristos, who began to outline the zoo's financial status. Mac glanced down at the printed Statement of Revenues and Expenditures that Claire had distributed. It went on for pages and, he had to admit, was the most detailed report he had ever seen. Cristos obviously knew his stuff. Mac flipped through the statistics on attendance income, departmental budgetary totals, and operating funds.

Halfway through the balance sheet, Mac thought for sure there was a typo. Under Assets was a figure so large it practically ran off the page. He read it a second time, and a third. He glanced over at Stewart. The manager seemed to be staring at the same page.

Then it hit him, H. L.'s estate. Mac had heard the former director had willed a huge sum to the zoo, but he hadn't known the exact amount. In fact, he'd never seen that many zeros in any column at any zoo. Good old H. L., he thought. Put his money where his principles were.

The head of marketing had begun his departmental report. A family night had been planned at the zoo, emphasizing wild-life education. Later that month Boston's symphony orchestra would perform a special concert in the amphitheater at dusk. The concert had sold out weeks in advance.

The meeting ground on as Keatings, the facilities department head, reported on the completion of a few projects. The new veterinary surgical suite was finished and would be dedicated next month. Excavation of Mohawk Lake for the moose exhibit in the North American habitat was to be done by the beginning of October so that Bogart, the adolescent male, could be moved into his permanent quarters before winter. Keatings's voice droned on.

The room was getting stuffy and the group squirmed restlessly in their chairs. Only Cristos seemed unaffected. Mac's attention drifted again. Other projects slated for the fiscal year were discussed, mostly projects H. L. had initiated before his death. Mac stared out the window. The pain in his left temple had become organized into a single pounding throb. Mention of the aviary caught his attention.

"As you know from Ed's memo," Keatings said, nodding toward Hargreve, "the aviary project has been put on hold. Now, let's see, the shark display tank will be arriving—"

"How long on hold?"

The group turned to look at Donald Stewart. Keatings, caught off guard, glanced at Hargreve.

"Until there is sufficient funding," Hargreve said, rhythmically tapping a Cross pen on the tabletop.

"So, indefinitely?"

"That's right." Hargreve signaled for Keatings to continue.

"You mean to tell me," Stewart said, flipping back to the balance sheet, "we acquire an endowment of that magnitude"—his finger stabbed the paper—"and a project that's been in the works for a year still gets scrapped?"

Hargreve's face had gone rigid. Cristos tipped his chair back on two legs and lit another cigarette. Keatings fixed his attention on a microscopic stain on his tie. The others seemed to be holding their breath.

Stewart waited, glaring unflinchingly at Hargreve from across the table.

"The, ah, former director made a number of decisions that did not incorporate good fiscal judgment. My job . . . our job"—he motioned toward Cristos, who was inspecting his cigarette's glowing tip—"is to get this ship seaworthy. That means scrapping some projects, using our finances to the maximum, and regrouping. A new flight house is not needed or necessary."

"And I suppose that a hundred and fifty thousand for refurbishing the Executive Suite is?" Stewart threw the report into the middle of the table.

Mac glanced at the others. Most had found a need to search for objects in their briefcases, jacket pockets, anywhere. No one looked up. Cristos flicked ashes in the direction of the ashtray, his face unreadable.

Stewart slowly looked around the room. His eyes met Mac's for a split, telling second. Mac knew what he was thinking. Hargreve had all these men neatly folded in his back pocket, all sixteen committee members. No, make that fifteen.

If Stewart stood up to Hargreve, the others would let him hang out to dry. Mac felt his stomach churn. He'd been out there before too, flapped into tatters, in fact.

Stewart rose slowly from his chair, contempt painted across his face, and strode from the room. The thick carpeting muffled the sound of the heavy mahogany door slamming shut.

Chapter 3

The red-naped widow bird struggled feebly against the large hand that gently but firmly restrained him. The newly arrived bird had flown into a glass viewing screen during its introduction to the zoo's flight cage, a common hazard to high-strung exotic birds. Mac was examining him for injuries.

He stretched out a wing, looking for signs of fracture. The little bird grabbed hold of the nearest offending finger and exerted as much pressure as the black beak could produce. Mac was sure it was trying to display its most fierce expression. The man grinned.

"Take it easy, fella, it'll be over in a minute." He ran a soft finger down the brilliant red head as the bird glowered defiantly up at him. This bird, while captive bred, was still as untamed as his wild relatives.

Mac inspected the bird's twelve-inch, elongated tail feathers despite the patient's vocal protests. Satisfied that there was no significant damage other than lost plumage, Mac returned the bird to its restraining cage.

"He's okay, just a little naked in spots. I don't think his ladies will mind," Mac said to the bird's keeper. "I want the glass screens to be washed down with Bon Ami right away. Total coverage. In two days, wipe off a few streaks. Then on Friday, take off half. Leave it that way till they're completely comfortable. He's lucky he didn't break his neck." The keeper nodded as he gathered up the cage.

Finished with the aviary unit, Mac drove the veterinary medical cart over to the video department to review last night's tapes. It had been the first night of Sienna's closed-circuit filming and he was anxious to see how she had fared.

The video cameras in both the gorilla and wolf areas were mounted on stationary tripods at floor level. One Panasonic WV-1410 black-and-white camera was aimed directly at the enclosure cage of Molly, the gorilla. With four 150-watt outdoor lights in light reflectors, her entire twenty-by-fifteen–foot night cage was illuminated. The floods gave just enough light to discern any sign of labor. Later, they would even be sufficient to document the birth.

For Sienna a lower amount of light was needed. Mac had ordered a Panasonic WV-1550 camera with one 60-watt bulb in a reflector. The bulb was angled so the light bounced off the wolf's recovery-room ceiling, giving a softer, less intrusive atmosphere.

Both cameras were hooked to separate VCRs, which recorded the entire shift. Each hour and half hour were logged with the tape's position. The docents watched the monitors closely during the night, hand-noting any unusual behavior. In the future Mac wanted to install a remote-controlled mount, zoom lens, and a microphone for sound.

Mac rewound the tape to the start of the previous night's shift. Molly was shown sleeping and later playing quietly with a piece of wood wool used as her bedding. Mac wanted to recognize Molly's labor immediately, since her last baby had died within hours, of a severe salmonella infection. Nothing looked unusual. He double-checked his calculations of her due date. It should be any time now.

Next he inserted Sienna's film into the VCR. The monitor flickered, then showed the wolf making a few tentative steps around the small enclosure. Her injured rear leg dangled uselessly. She made no attempt to touch it to the ground—the first important sign of improvement. It could take weeks for her to show signs of strengthening.

What concerned him now was an angry-looking three-inch laceration just above her left eye. It had been cleaned and sutured, but the wound was beginning to look damp around the edges. From the film it was difficult to tell if this was just normal oozing or the beginning of an infection. Mac needed a closer look. Once again he grappled with having to treat from a distance. He rubbed his sore ribs from yesterday's encounter with Sheba and dismissed any idea of personally handling the wolf. He'd have to tranquilize her and she had already had a lot of anesthesia over the past few weeks. Mac made a note to check on the wound again later.

Ten minutes later he pulled up to the concrete fortress that housed the pachyderms and carnivores in the winter months. Bobby, a six-year-old African elephant, needed attention for a foot injury caused by the enclosure's cement flooring.

Reaching the treatment area, Mac paused and watched the young animal. Bobby's huge ears fanned gently as he moved, an instantly recognizable badge of his African heritage. Friendly and agreeable at this young age, Bobby would soon grow to be close to six tons of restless, curious bull energy. Because of their great strength and unpredictability during mating season, only a handful of males are kept in American zoos. Koko, Rockland's resident adult African male, had more than once earned the respect of the keepers.

Mac opened his medical bag and squatted down next to the bars of the treatment pen for a closer look at the injury. Just learning his commands, Bobby would have to be helped to maintain the foot-up position Mac needed.

Decker appeared around the corner, carrying a huge bale of hay on his shoulder. "Mind giving me a hand with this guy?" Mac asked. Decker set the eighty-pound bundle down as if it were a grocery sack and took an ankus off its spot on the wall.

The keeper gently placed the blunt hook end of the prod into the broad ear of the elephant. He gave the order for the elephant to lift his foot. Bobby flapped his ears and stood with all four feet planted firmly on the ground. Decker repeated the command, louder. The young elephant flapped again in response. Mac put his head down and tried to hide his grin.

Decker reached over for a second ankus, placing it against the underside of the elephant's leg. Giving a tug on the ear, the keeper boomed the command, the sound a hollow echo inside the huge building. Bobby promptly lifted his trunk, circus style.

"He's got your number, Decker."

"Yeah, these guys can outmaneuver anything on the Serengeti, and he's playing dumb."

"You used to be a guide in Kenya, I heard. How'd you get into that?"

Bobby finally agreed to cooperate and obligingly lifted his foot. Mac took a large hoof knife and began trimming away pieces of split foot pad.

Decker shrugged. "A guy offered me a job, so I took it."

"That last trip must have been a bitch." Mac looked up at the burly keeper. At 200 pounds and six feet tall Mac considered himself to be a big man, but compared to Decker he looked malnourished. Decker was solid muscle and looked accustomed to taking care of himself.

"Death, life . . . that's all it is out there, anyway," Decker replied. "You done?"

Mac applied Koppertox to the wound and nodded. He watched Decker lead the elephant out through the twelve-foot enclosure doors as if it were a golden retriever. It wasn't that

Decker was unfriendly, but the man didn't exactly make him feel all warm and chummy, either. Mac couldn't imagine being a lot of African miles from nowhere with only Decker to talk to. You'd die of the silence.

Decker was like men he'd seen all over the world, living on the fringes of society. Men without ties. Men who make a point of having only a present, no past, no future.

•   •   •

Hargreve had just finished the paperwork to transfer money into a discretionary account when his office door opened with such force that it bounced off the wall, the knob leaving a dent in the new grass-cloth wallcovering. Stewart stood in the door brandishing a crumpled memo.

"What the hell is this, Hargreve? 'All budgetary decisions must be jointly approved by the director and the chief financial officer.' You eliminating my job?"

Hargreve slowly took off his reading glasses. "Take it easy. I have no intention of eliminating your job. It's just that the zoo would be better served with its financial decisions being made by people who have the big picture." Hargreve tried to look confident. Stewart always made him nervous. "This is a big business. The zoo takes in over three million dollars a year, not chicken feed that can be frittered away. The animals and our membership depend on our ability to provide what is very expensive upkeep. I'm not just trying to protect the present condition of the zoo, but I want to improve it."

It sounded good, even fiscally responsible. Exactly what Hargreve, as the director, should be doing. And the director knew anyone but Stewart would have swallowed it. Hargreve spun the diamond ring around on his finger. "Now if you want to talk about this rationally, come in and close the door." He gestured with forced casualness in the direction of one of the high-backs.

"Very smooth. You are that, Edward. . . . But *I* know you're up to something and *you* better know, pal, I'm onto this," Stewart said through clenched teeth as he spun on his heel and strode from the office.

Claire pretended to be absorbed with her work at the computer as Stewart roared by. Hargreve took a deep breath and wiped his sweaty palms on his handkerchief.

• • •

Mac took the shortcut through the connecting underground tunnel that ran from the pachyderm to the carnivore compound. Used primarily during the difficult New England winters, the passageway had become cluttered and dirty during the intervening months. He picked his way through the disorder.

There was only one surgery scheduled for today, but Mac had been trying to put it off as long as possible. His patient was the most notorious animal at the zoo, Duke, a 600-pound Siberian tiger.

Duke had the healthy respect of all the keepers. Big, nervous, aggressive, he was one animal they all felt could be instantly lethal if he ever got loose. From what little Mac had seen of the tiger he had to agree. Duke was a lit fuse burning to home.

Mac had seen the Bad Boy, as they called him, bend the heavy-gauge chain link of his enclosure with his teeth as if he were biting through straw. This habit had finally broken off a tooth, requiring today's root canal.

Nat Watermann had Duke confined in the cat compound's holding cage. Waiting for the vet hadn't improved Duke's disposition. Mac took out a blowgun and loaded the tranquilizer into the barrel.

"What jungle you find that in?"

Mac grinned. "It's quieter than a gun. Doesn't get them so stirred up. Most of these guys can spot a rifle a mile off. Drug works better if they're not all uptight."

Although that was relatively speaking. M99 was one of the newest tranquilizers out. It dropped them in seconds, with few side effects.

Mac aimed the barrel of the two-foot blow gun and hit the massive animal in the flank with the first shot. The cat whirled, angered, with lips raised, broken tooth exposed. Within moments the tiger began to crumple slowly down onto the cement floor. It took seven keepers plus Mac to put Duke on a tarp and drag him out into the treatment area. Mac quickly began to work on the cat's canine tooth. Watermann knelt at the tiger's head, keeping a close watch on its breathing.

The tooth drilled and the exposed root removed, Mac packed it and finished off the dental work. He helped the keepers drag the limp animal back into the ten-foot-square holding cage. Duke would stay there until they were sure that he had fully recovered. Mac raised the blowgun again and delivered the reversing drug, M5050, right on target.

Stewart whistled in appreciation from the doorway. "Remind me not to challenge you to darts."

In seconds, Duke was back on his feet, unsteady but standing. Mac marveled again at the speed and effectiveness of the two drugs. Knock them out and then bring them back, whenever you want, presto. Mac stuck the blow gun back into his bag.

"I want to go over my ideas with you for the red wolf exhibit, when you have a minute, Mac."

"I'm going there now to check on Sienna. Walk over with me," Mac replied.

The two men started in the direction of the recently expanded wolf habitat. Large boulders, natural woodland plantings, and a stream had been manufactured into the environment. Stewart had planned and developed the exhibit, attempting to make it as close to naturally wild as possible.

Having thirteen of only 160 remaining red wolves in the world made Rockland Zoo vital to their existence. The wolves had once populated much of the southern United States, but man had hunted them past the point of their survival, not realizing the important role they played in a balanced ecology. Mac had first heard of the red wolf's plight when it was placed on the endangered species list in 1973. One day, he hoped, the wolves would again be numerous enough to be released back into the wild. But man would have to be compassionate. And in the meantime, Stewart had been waging a battle with evolution.

"I just compared the dental mold you took of Meke's pups with those of the first wolves, which were brought in eight years ago." Stewart seemed unusually depressed. "Geez, I think we're losing it here. Pretty sure there's some change. I want to take some molds from our other litter."

Mac turned and opened the door of Sienna's confinement area. The manager didn't seem himself. "Sure. No problem. I'll just take a mold whenever I knock 'em down. What's up?"

"All this time in captivity's changing them. Same as those wolves down in New Mexico. Not having to hunt's altering the shape of the muzzle. Making it shorter, more domestic. Less depth. Less width to orbit ratio. Meke's pups are showing it already—not much, but it's there."

"And if the wolves can't hunt, we can't release them." Another man-made defeat. "What can we do?"

"Stop or cut down on the commercially prepared dog food. Give them access to hunting . . . challenge 'em," Stewart said.

"How about we put in some movable boulders and fallen logs. Change the decor every week. Drop in a few meals on the hoof—after visiting hours—so they get the feel of providing for themselves. It won't be a moose or a deer, but at least they can practice a little."

Stewart stared wide-eyed in excitement. He clapped the vet on the shoulder. "You got style, MacIntire. Think Hargreve will go for it?"

"It's a medical necessity," Mac said, grinning mischievously.

The men approached Sienna's enclosure. "I really need to get a closer look at that laceration," Mac said. The wound looked worse than it had that morning. A thick yellow goo oozed from the lower corner just above the eye.

"No problem, come in behind me."

"What?"

The manager opened the gate and stepped inside. Mac stood tentatively inside the enclosure, ready to leap to safety. A female wolf, although significantly smaller in body mass than a male, could still be a formidable opponent. At seventy pounds and six feet in length, with her jaw she could exert close to 200 pounds of pressure per square inch. Certainly enough to break a man's arm and probably tear it from the socket.

Luckily the stories of wolf attacks were largely exaggerated. In fact, not a single case of wolf attack has ever been recorded in North America. The only documented cases are by Russian wolves against men on horseback or in horse-drawn wagons, most likely as the wolves went after the horses. There is even a theory that the wolves might have been rabid. Even so, it paid to be careful with any wild animal. And Sienna's intense gold stare certainly inspired respect.

Mac watched, astonished, as Stewart approached and squatted down. Sienna, who had backed off, as most wolves do when approached by a human, came forward again in a bound. Mac involuntarily tensed until he realized the leap was in joy. Complete, body-twisting, tail-thumping joy. Sienna fell over on her back and kicked her legs in the air, exposing her belly for Stewart to rub. Mac, in all his years, had never seen such a display of unbridled affection from a wolf.

"Come on in, Mac, she'll let me hold her head long enough for you to take a look."

Mac slowly approached the female and angled around to see

the wound. It was infected and needed antibiotics, full spectrum. Luckily it had not spread down into the orbital area. The two men let themselves out of the enclosure.

"Are they all like that with you?"

"Most of them. As long as you play by their rules, you're fine. Of course Toka, the dominant male, would never lower himself to such an undignified display, but he's still my guy." Stewart brushed a large paw print off the front of his khaki uniform. "With the next litter, if we're going to be a part of the Florida island release, I'm not going to get so close. Real hands off. They need to be wary of man. Unfortunately."

Mac sighed. It seemed wherever man and animal ran into each other, the animal was holding a fixed hand. If man were at the mercy of a predator more powerful than himself, then he might learn something, Mac thought.

Stewart locked the enclosure gate. Every gate in the zoo was secured by at least one lock, sometimes more. Safety was a major issue but even so, working in a zoo could be extremely dangerous.

"So what'd you think of our little session with the director?" Stewart asked.

Mac hesitated.

"That avian project should never have been canned and I'm going to fight it," Stewart continued. He looked him straight in the eye. "Listen, Mac, I don't know what's going on, but Hargreve and Cristos are up to something. And I'm not going to just sit here. You with me or what?"

"What are they up to?"

Stewart fidgeted from one foot to the other. "I'm not exactly sure yet. I have a suspicion . . . but I need to check a few things out before I say. But I know Hargreve, and he's trouble, always has been. So are you with me or not?"

"Listen, I'm the new kid on the block here. My two-cents aren't worth a damn, especially with Hargreve." Mac snapped his treatment bag shut. "I'm behind you in theory but I'm not interested in getting back on the firing line. I've had all the politics I can stomach. I came here to get away from that."

"If I'm right, it's more than just some boardroom infighting." Stewart looked away. Something was clearly bothering him. "Hey, Gerald Durrell's coming to Boston next week. Want to go hear him?"

Mac felt his stomach do a perfect reverse half-gainer. The judges would have been proud. It had been months since he had heard that name. He had hoped it would be years.

"Small world."

Stewart looked at him.

"My, ah, wife studied with him. At his preserve in the English Channel, 'bout ten years ago."

"Wife? I didn't know you were married."

"Past tense." Mac swallowed hard.

"If she was connected to Durrell, especially back then, she's got to be a trailblazer. He was yelling for zoos to help with conservation thirty years ago. Everybody thought he was some kind of nut. Now they say he was right. Your wife must be a handful."

"Biopolitics was her specialty. Sara did a lot of environmental impact studies for various organizations. That's how she met Durrell—and how I met her. I had been helping a conservation group resist a buy-out from a mining company. She did the impact study. Found some pretty nasty stuff. . . . But she was like a little terrier, completely fearless and totally oblivious to the personal dangers."

Stewart was watching him closely. "You look like a man still in love."

Mac took a deep breath. Five years and it was still hard, the explaining. "I guess you never—"

Stewart's walkie-talkie blasted Watermann's urgent request for help. A gate door had jammed at the herbivore complex and a giraffe was attacking a younger male. Mac and Stewart took off for the area at a dead run.

An adult giraffe can kick forward with the lethal force of a thirty-miles-an-hour car crash. The little one was trying its best to avoid the flying hooves. As he retreated, he moved farther back into a corner of the exercise yard. Without help he would have been defenseless in minutes. Watermann and four other keepers cautiously circled around from the side, unable to get into a good position.

Mac yanked a tranquilizer gun out of his bag and began to load quickly. Bringing down a fourteen-foot-tall animal in an exercise yard was tricky. If the animal staggered in the wrong direction, it could fall into the retaining moat, the glass viewing panels, or another animal.

Inserting the drug cartridge into the high-powered pistol, Mac tried to seat it into the chamber. The cartridge refused to engage. The big giraffe lunged forward, kicking viciously at the younger animal, who scrambled back in fear. Only seconds were left. With his thumb Mac forced the cartridge down the shaft. He pulled back on the safety. It wouldn't budge.

"It's jammed," he yelled.

Decker appeared on the far side of the big giraffe. He motioned to Watermann to move forward. The other keepers positioned themselves in line with him. Watermann covered the ground in two leaps and faced the big male as Decker rushed at the giraffe from the other side.

Swinging his jacket above his head, Decker dove in between the two giraffes as the little one cowered against the enclosure wall. The sleeve of the jacket arced up, grazing the muzzle of the big male as Decker shouted and waved. Watermann and the other keepers, following his lead, stepped in behind, forming a wall of noise and confusion. Startled, the old male backed quickly away, stamping his feet in frustration. He lumbered off into another section of the habitat, just as the gun's safety clicked neatly into the firing position. Mac disarmed it and tossed it into his treatment bag in disgust as the keepers herded the little male into another paddock.

"Damn gun," Mac said to Watermann, who had reappeared from inside the paddock. "Decker sure showed up at the right time. Now there's a cowboy."

Watermann wiped a layer of dust from his sweating face, leaving a series of dark streaks. "He's either the bravest man I know or he has ice water for blood." The keeper shook his head and walked back into the yard.

That was twice Mac had screwed up in two days, and he didn't like it, especially when lives were at stake. Decker rounded the corner as Mac turned to go.

"Thanks for your help. Could have been a nasty mess."

"Forget it. Just a matter of knowing who you can intimidate."

Mac watched Decker's muscular back walk away. This was no phony macho act. The man seemed immune to fear.

•   •   •

Mac knew he couldn't put it off any longer. He had to finish the discussion with Hargreve about the wolf breeding program. Without the director's okay, the necessary Species Survival Plan applications couldn't be filed with the national zoo organization. Even so, Mac purposely took his time getting to the Executive Suite.

Claire had her back to him, filing a stack of papers, as he entered the office. She had on a navy two-piece business suit that followed the contours of her body. The jacket was fitted at the waist, stopping just at the top of the soft curve of hip. She looked small enough to get your arms around, and then some. He thought about that and liked the idea. Claire turned.

"Poor thing."

"What?"

"Whatever you swallowed."

Mac felt himself starting to blush. "Oh, uh, Stewart just told me this joke . . . forget it." This was not going well. "The boss busy?"

"He's not here. Rubbing elbows with the in people, you know." She glanced down at the appointment book. "I can get you in tomorrow morning first thing. How long you need?"

"I have to go over the wolf breeding proposal. Maybe half an hour total?"

Claire jotted it down in the book, without looking up. "So you going to hang in there with us? Ship's pretty rocky."

"I've got great balance."

"That's good. I don't know, the way things are going between Hargreve and Stewart, well, it was never like this before. . . ." She settled onto the edge of the desk, the knee-length straight skirt moving up to show a bit more leg. "So which lifeboat are you in?"

"Lifeboat?"

"You kinda have to pick a lifeboat when the ship's going down."

"Think I'd rather swim for it."

She stared at him for a two-second count. "Better get on your trunks, I have the feeling you're gonna get wet."

It wasn't what she said, maybe it was the way she said it, that reminded him of Sara. Responsibility to a cause. Defending your principles. Getting off the fence and taking a stand.

Mac turned abruptly and headed for the door as he asked, "What time tomorrow? Nine?"

He didn't wait for her response, his stride double its usual reach.

•   •   •

His stomach frantically signaling for its overdue lunch, Mac walked over to the cafeteria, where most of the keepers were taking their union break. Stewart usually showed up around this time and Mac wanted to be sure there were no hard feelings between them. Collecting a generic sandwich and glass of tasteless punch, he picked a far booth and waited.

Half an hour later Mac gave up and brushed the last few remaining crumbs onto a paper napkin. He wanted to go find Stewart, but he knew it was just a halfhearted excuse to ignore the stacks of paperwork waiting for him back in his office. He resignedly heaved himself to his feet.

Entering his cluttered office, Mac pushed clear a space on the desk and sat down, teeth gritted, already bored. Methodically he began to work his way through chart after medical chart.

Four hours later, an erratic heap of updated records encircled his feet. He closed the last one, rubbed his stinging eyes, and glanced at his watch. The sun had been replaced by darkness and dinner hour had long since come and gone.

Mac reached for the walkie-talkie. What he wanted now was an ice-cold ale and a steak, thick, medium rare. Maybe Stewart would join him.

"Unit Ninety-four to Unit Eighty-one. Over."

The walkie-talkie hummed. Mac repeated the call. Silence. Stewart must have already left.

Mac walked out of the office into the warm evening air. He could hear the animals in the North American Region settling down. In warm weather a number of species were allowed to sleep outside at night. He stopped at the sight of a herd of shaggy bison hunkered down on the gently rolling hills made to resemble the American plains. Their huge shapes stood out as inky dark silhouettes against the summer-scorched grass. He could imagine the awe of early settlers seeing the massive lumps as they circled their wagons at the end of the day.

A trio of dry leaves scurried across the asphalt sidewalk, propelled by the autumn breeze. In the full moon he could see clearly even without a flashlight. Stuffing his broad hands into his pockets, he ambled toward the guard booth at the zoo's front exit.

Security guard Jeff Vincent was tipped back on two legs of the desk chair, reading the evening paper, as Mac entered the office.

"Hi, Doc, burning the night oil again?"

"Stewart left already?"

Jeff glanced over at the rack of time cards. "Nope, he's still on the grounds. You need him?"

"Wanted to go for a beer and couldn't raise him." Mac leaned back against the doorframe. "Maybe I'll go check the wolf compound. Bet his radio's on the blink."

"I haven't had a beer in weeks. Trying to work off a few. Even started jogging my rounds." Jeff grinned, patting a barely rounded abdomen. "Say, wouldn't Stewart be at that meeting? The whole Development bunch's over in the main building." He looked at the wall clock. "Started over an hour ago."

After all that had been going on with Hargreve, Mac knew Stewart would be at the meeting. Mac headed over to the administration building. As he opened the door, voices drifted down from somewhere upstairs. Taking the stairs, he stuck his head into the first open door.

Seated at a rectangular table were twelve members of the Development Committee. Cristos was in mid-sentence, reporting on the capital funding of some project Mac didn't catch. Hargreve sat opposite him, arms folded, jiggling an Italian brown wing-tip shoe. Hilton Locke sat closest to the door. Mac didn't know the other members. One chair at the far end of the table stood empty.

Locke turned at Mac's appearance at the door. "Dr. MacIntire, can I help you?" he whispered.

"Sorry, I was looking for Donald Stewart," Mac whispered back, crouching down.

"Never showed up. I'm surprised. But if he comes, I'll tell him you're looking for him."

Mac nodded and backed away from the doorway. That was odd. Stewart said he was going to fight Hargreve about the avian project—and this committee was command center and battlefield combined. Mac glanced at his watch. It was now 9:00 P.M.

Puzzled, he left the building and started toward the parking lot. Something bothered him. Something more than just another empty stomach. Stewart wouldn't miss that meeting, of all meetings. He was the type of guy who'd go even if he didn't have to.

Mac changed his mind and cut back toward the farthest part of the North American Region. From this angle he would come to the rear of the wolf enclosure. If Stewart acted as if he wanted to be alone, Mac could leave without being seen.

He was halfway there when the sound came from ahead of him in the darkness. Low, it swelled and floated, vibrating, and was joined by others, rising to an eerie crescendo that lingered on the night air.

The small hairs on the back of his neck stood up as something almost physical put its hand into his chest and began to squeeze. He knew that feeling. Mac broke into a run as the wolves continued their strange and haunting song.

As he skidded around the far end of the darkened wolf enclosure, he could hear movement inside the habitat, the sound of wolves, active, too active. Reaching the entrance gate, Mac peered into the heavily wooded lot. He fished his flashlight out of his back pocket and shone the light into the enclosure.

Two of the smaller females were pacing just inside the doorway. They were clearly agitated, spinning around to face him, lips curling back to expose thin rows of shimmering white.

Mac raced farther down the path, the moon illuminating

everything in stark silver. His heart beat him breathless. Beaming the light around the main viewing area, he at last saw Toka, the lead male, standing at full attention. Mac had found the source of the sound.

At first he thought the wolf was alerting the others to his arrival but then realized Toka hadn't even seen him, or didn't care.

The big male lifted his black muzzle to the sky, and the sound swelled, floating up from his open mouth. Mac had never heard it before, in the wild or in captivity. The others stood still and joined the lament.

Fear gripped Mac with icy hands. A momentary flash of memory, of Sara's doctor walking out of the operating room, slowly. He knew now, as he knew then, that something was wrong, terribly wrong.

Toka, seeing Mac, moved to the side, his gold eyes reflecting in the light's beam. The rest of the pack, shadows, faded into the underbrush. Toka took two steps forward and stood over a long dark patch on the ground. The male raised his lone voice in haunting soliloquy.

In front of the glass viewing panel Stewart lay sprawled, face down, a bucket of glass cleaner beside him. Mac flung himself at the fence, clambering over the top military fashion, oblivious to the danger. Toka joined the others in the underbrush and watched the big vet closely.

Grabbing Stewart by the shoulder, Mac gently rolled him over. A window squeegee fell from the manager's plastic-gloved right hand. Stewart's mangled and bloody left forearm trailed across his chest, underlining the gaping hole where his throat had once been. Wine-dark blood soaked slowly into the hardpacked earth.

Fumbling for the walkie-talkie at his belt, Mac put in an emergency call, his voice shaking uncontrollably. Jeff Vincent's voice responded, unnerved.

Mac reached out gently and wiped away a smudge of blood from the dead man's cheek. Sitting down in the dirt beside his friend, he put his head in his hands and waited for help.

• • •

Mac watched in shocked silence as police swarmed around the grounds. The floodlights made the men look pale and surrealistic in the stark brilliance. Mac had barely been able to stumble to the controls that lowered the dividing gate, creating a twenty-by-forty–foot smaller area at the entrance, effectively shutting the wolves away from the scene of the investigation.

Kirby was motioning to a couple of uniformed officers. Standing off to one side, Watermann was talking quietly to another. Mac sat motionless on one of the benches beside the glass viewing panel.

Stewart lay just on the other side, a black plastic sheet pulled back, as the medical examiner coordinated the removal of the body. A small stream of blood had trailed down Stewart's left arm from a perfect horseshoe imprint of teeth marks, running over the cuff of the plastic glove, across its thin powder coating, and down between the third and fourth fingers. The blood had dotted a small circle in the dust.

The flash of a camera punctuated the night. Mac felt as if he were only partially there, another larger part held in suspended animation a million miles away. He stared blankly at the manager's body.

"You touch anything, Doc?" the medical examiner asked as he and Kirby walked up.

"I rolled him over . . . when I found him. He was already dead."

"Face down?"

"What? Oh, yes," Mac replied, running a trembling hand through his hair. "Holding a squeegee. Must have been cleaning the glass. It was still wet when I got here." Mac wanted to stand up but he didn't trust his legs. "I didn't touch anything else—oh, I lowered the dividing gate and turned on the night floods."

"Why would Mr. Stewart have been wearing surgeon's gloves?"

"It's general practice. We wear them to prepare food, clean equipment, lots of things. We work with a lot of strong disinfectants," he finished numbly.

The medical examiner jotted down a few notes in his book, nodded, and walked back to his assistants.

"That's it?" Kirby asked.

"That's my story."

"A manager was washing windows?" Kirby asked, with a note of disbelief.

"He spent hours here. It wasn't unusual for him to even shovel the place out—he was that kind of guy." A lump suddenly appeared mid-throat. Mac swallowed, hard. It wouldn't go down.

Over Kirby's shoulder he watched as the medical examiner carefully removed the plastic surgeon's gloves from the body. He held each glove gingerly. An assistant opened an evidence bag and the gloves were carefully dropped into it. A puff of translucent glove powder rose from the bag before it was sealed. The medical examiner wiped his hands onto his black trouser leg and then put the squeegee into another bag. Mac turned away as the assistants hoisted Stewart's body onto a morgue stretcher.

"Sorta biting off the hand that feeds 'em, huh?" Kirby said.

"What?"

"The wolves. Ironic, isn't it?"

"What are you saying, Kirby?"

"It's obvious. The wolves killed him while he was inside

cleaning. And that, Doctor, makes them man killers in my book." Something flickered in the far back of the detective's flat gray eyes.

Mac didn't consider himself aggressive. He could certainly take care of himself, 'Nam had proved that, but he never looked for trouble. But something right now made Mac want to take hold of Kirby's soft, flabby neck. Right where the extra paunchy layer of skin folded down over the cop's unstarched collar. Take hold of it, with both hands, hard.

Mac stood up. "You're nuts, Kirby. Dead wrong. If you think those wolves had anything to do with Stewart's death—. He was their alpha leader. They'd never attack their pack leader. No way."

"Oh, so a man left that set of teeth marks on the victim's arm and then ripped his throat out?"

"I . . . I don't know. But I do know that wolves don't attack their leader. And they seldom attack a man, for that matter, even in the wild. Unless they're rabid. Something just doesn't fit here." Mac rubbed a hand across the day's worth of dark beard stubble.

"If you're so sure, then tell me something, Dr. MacIntire. How do you explain the blood on the front of that big one over there?" Kirby pointed through the fencing.

Across the muzzle and down the chest of Toka ran streaks of blood, unmistakable, even in that lighting. Mac stood in stunned silence.

Pulling out his notebook, Kirby jotted down a few notes. "Course we can't be sure which one attacked him, probably a joint project." Kirby snorted. "I'll have to get a court order in the morning. What's the name of that big one?"

Mac was only half hearing. "What one? . . . ah, Toka. Court order? For what?"

"Their disposal. Law says even zoos can't have animals that

are considered uncontrollable hazards. You most likely will be able to decide how you want to do it."

Rage hit Mac like a blast of red-hot exhaust. He stepped toward the policeman, putting his face within inches of the other man's. Veins bulged along both sides of his neck as he fought the urge to grab the detective. "Listen, Kirby. I'm not going to put these wolves down. Not for you, not for the court. Got it? They didn't do it, it's not how they'd act. I *know* wolves. They're my specialty. Stewart went in and out of there at will, hundreds of times."

The cop moved back slightly. The vet was right on the edge. "Take it easy, fella."

"There's only about a hundred left in the world and you want to put them down? No way are they a threat to the public."

"Listen, Doc, I understand this has been a shock. But we're dealing with wild animals here. For Christ's sake, they've killed somebody. I knew something like this was gonna happen. Now it has, and it's my job to clean it up." The detective stuffed the worn notebook back into his rear pocket and turned on his heel. Over his shoulder he added, "It's straight-cut, MacIntire, they're man killers. And I'm going to recommend your Board of Directors handles it before I get a court order to do it for them."

Mac felt desperation move in where the anger had been.

"Kirby, wait. Wait." The detective stopped and turned back. "I can prove it . . . I can. But give me a couple of days. If I can't, then I'll put them down. Deal?"

Kirby stared at him. A long, steady appraisal. Mac held his breath. He wasn't sure about Kirby. Kirby might have had some compassion years ago. Before the job or something had ground it into a slick veneer of callous indifference. Mac couldn't really blame him; cops can't afford to feel sorry for anyone. It gets in the way of the job. But the wolves' lives depended on one last little spark. "Come on, Kirby . . . ," he said softly.

The detective took three steps toward him and pointed his finger up into Mac's face. "If your directors agree to put them down voluntarily, within forty-eight hours, then I'll wait to get the court order. If you can't prove anything, then that's it. I'll take those suckers down personally. You got it?"

Mac nodded. His knees felt like rubber. He held out his hand to the cop. "One more thing, Detective." Kirby looked exasperated. "Don't release the news of Stewart's death until tomorrow evening. Give me a head start?"

"Jesus Christ, MacIntire, I'm a cop. It's my job to run this investigation, not pat your ass. I can't delay anything."

"I'm not saying delay your investigation. It's just that, well, if there is someone behind this, I need time. We both want the same thing, Kirby—to find out who or what killed Stewart. Right? Just don't give it to the press until tomorrow?"

The detective stared at him for a minute. "I'm not promising anything," he said and strode off, gesturing to his men. The uniformed policemen continued to search the area carefully. Mac could tell from Kirby's expression he thought it was a waste of time.

• • •

Jeff Vincent stepped into the Development Committee's meeting with two uniformed policemen close behind. Hargreve stopped talking abruptly. All eyes turned to look at the young man shifting nervously at the doorway.

"What is it, Vincent?"

"Mr. Hargreve, there's been an accident."

"Can't this wait?" he said, irritated.

"I'm afraid not. Donald Stewart is dead."

The room inhaled collectively. Hargreve dropped his pen. For a few seconds the only sound was Cristos's lighter rasping forth another flame.

Hargreve stopped at his office briefly on the way down to

meet with the police. He had a bad feeling about this. He placed his leather briefcase on the high-back chair and flipped on the table light. Tucked into the desk blotter was a folded piece of white notepaper addressed to him. Inside it read, "The lion's share is mine."

Chapter 4

The ringing had been going on for some time when Mac finally struggled up from the depths. He groped, bleary-eyed, in the direction of the alarm clock.

A vague something nagged at him, a sense of something wrong, way back in the sleep-sodden gray mush that was this morning's brain. Mac shoved his head back under the oversized pillow. He just wanted to sleep uninterrupted, a feeling he had had before. Blunted, dull, his mind refused to function. A distinct ache brewed where neurons should have been firing. He tried to dive back into the warm, blissful abyss.

He was almost there, almost oblivious, when last night's horror flooded back on him with the force of a blow to the solar plexus. He rolled over onto his back, gulping air. Grief and disbelief erased the last vestiges of sleep.

Stewart was dead. Mac rolled over and peered at the clock. It showed a few minutes past 7:00 A.M.

He crawled, half fell out of the queen-sized bed and staggered to the bathroom. He turned the shower on hot and hard, looked at his face in the rapidly fogging mirror, and was startled. He groaned, glad no one was there to see him bearded and haggard. It was the only benefit of sleeping solo.

He stayed in until the hot water ran out. It scalded away the dirt and mental cobwebs but did nothing for his anger. He had an hour before his appointment with Hargreve. Usually he went in early to do rounds, but today he had to organize his thoughts. He had to convince Hargreve to back him against Kirby, to contest destroying the wolves. The zoo could fight it.

'Nam had taught him not to trust coincidence. Whatever looked innocent probably wasn't. And, right now, the only thing he could believe was the innocence of the wolves. Nothing else about the past few days seemed to add up.

A poisonous snake freak—at least anyone still breathing—would know the difference between a tree snake and a deadly mamba. Listing both snakes as harmless had to have been cold-bloodedly intentional. A deception as effective as a time bomb.

Both deaths were too accidental, and it made Mac uneasy. In fact, it gave him the same squirmy feeling he had had in that Saigon bar—right before the ticking stopped.

Mac rummaged through a pile of cardboard boxes that were still stacked around the one-bedroom apartment. There hadn't been any pressing need to unpack. He found the Mr. Coffee machine and the lone can of coffee sitting in an otherwise barren kitchen cabinet. Rinsing out an old Dunkin' Donuts cup and waiting for the coffee to brew, he looked around. Pictures leaned haphazardly against stark white walls, hammer and nails lying forgotten on the floor. An aging sofa kept the boxes company in the hollow living room. He hadn't even found the silverware yet. Pouring himself a cup, Mac stirred the coffee with the end of a pencil. Taking three blistering gulps, he went back into the rumpled bedroom and started to get ready.

●　　　●　　　●

Hargreve's door was closed when Mac entered the Executive Suite. Mac thought the room was empty until he saw Claire standing by the office window. Something about her shoulders told him she was crying. He walked up behind her.

"You okay?"

Claire swiped at her eyes with a soggy Kleenex. She looked exactly like he felt.

"I just can't believe it. He was such a nice guy. . . ." Tears welled up and spilled down to her jaw.

Mac put an arm around her shoulders. She turned, leaning her head against his chest, her body shaking from suppressed sobs, warm tears soaking through to his skin. He muttered reassuring nothings to make them both feel better. They pretended it did.

Claire pulled back and smiled weakly up at him. "I've never lost a friend before."

Mac nodded. He had.

From behind Hargreve's door voices became louder. Claire hastily wiped her face with a remaining dry edge of tissue and stepped behind her desk as the door opened. "Yes, Dr. MacIntire, Mr. Hargreve is just finishing with Mr. Locke. He'll be with you in a minute," she said stiffly.

Hilton Locke came out of the office looking grim, nodding curtly at Mac as he passed. Mac could see Hargreve through the open door, sitting behind his desk and staring into space. Hargreve looked even worse than Claire did.

The director motioned Mac into the room. "Hilt and I were just discussing this situation. Have a seat."

Mac eased down into the leather chair. He trusted his instincts and they were flashing a full alert.

"I spent most of the night here with the police. The situation is not good. But we will try to defuse this situation as quickly as we can, with as little publicity as possible. I think the police want to wrap this up as quickly as we do."

Mac bristled at the way Hargreve kept referring to *the situ-*

ation, as if Stewart's death was merely an administrative inconvenience. He glanced down and was surprised to find his knuckles white, his hand in a viselike grip on the chair's arm.

Mac cleared his throat. "Listen . . . Ed, last night Detective Kirby claimed he would get a court order for the disposal of the wolves. Now you and I know there's always an inherent danger with keeping any wild animal—"

"Quite right," Hargreve interrupted. "Of course it will be better if the zoo handles the matter voluntarily. No point dragging our dirty laundry through the courts. Hilt has already spoken by phone with the other Board members and they agree."

"To what?"

"The disposal. I'd like you to be in charge. However you want . . . by injection, I would imagine?"

Mac stared, speechless. He forced himself to remain calm. "Mr. Hargreve, the red wolf is an endangered species. To put down the eight percent of them that we have here at the zoo is . . . unthinkable. Most of the animals out there"—Mac gestured toward the window—"are potential man killers. For God's sake, they're *wild.*"

Hargreve remained impassive. "I understand the impact this will have on the species. But I have a greater responsibility. The zoo is not exempt from the law. Plus we need to think of how this will affect our reputation."

"Who are you kidding—it'll double our attendance," Mac said cynically. "When that game park's keeper was eaten by the polar bear, attendance soared. People were curious to see where it had happened. But that's not the point here. Let's say the wolves did kill Stewart. If we put them down because they behaved according to the laws of nature, we might as well put down every last animal out there. All creatures have the hunting instinct, even man. But for the animals it's their only means of survival.

"And we have a moral responsibility to protect our animals. We've taken them from the wild and now we must be their guardians. Besides," he continued, "it's pretty obvious Kirby has a certain prejudice against the zoo."

"Very inspiring, Doctor, but the Board has already approved the action."

Mac felt himself losing his restraint. "I can prove the wolves didn't do it," he blurted. It was Hargreve's turn to stare. "I told Kirby that last night. This is not normal pack behavior. I think"—Mac took a deep breath—"something, or someone, else killed Stewart. In fact, doesn't Joanne's death strike you as a little coincidental?"

Hargreve went still. "Why do you say that?"

"Something doesn't work here. Especially Stewart's death. The animal behavior is wrong, the attack is wrong. Nothing fits. Wolves hunt as a team. If the pack had turned on Stewart, we would have found him in tiny bits and pieces. That didn't happen. But I need time . . . ," Mac finished lamely.

"You can prove it?" Hargreve nervously spun his ring around his finger.

Mac hesitated. He'd have to play this to the hilt.

"I haven't got it all worked out yet, but if I'm right, the murderer might kill again. Face it, Donald Stewart was just a nice guy—not the type that makes mortal enemies."

Mac watched Hargreve closely. A shadow of an expression flickered across the director's face. It seemed to hit home.

"How much time would you need?"

"Kirby agreed to forty-eight hours."

Hargreve got up and walked over to the window. Looking out he said, "I would like to be certain of who or what killed Stewart." He turned. Hargreve was silhouetted against the bright sky, and Mac couldn't see his face. "All right, I'll get the Board to go along with this. But that's all, MacIntire. And you report only to me. If you can't prove anything, the wolves go down in two days, at closing time. Not a minute longer and no arguments."

Mac nodded, breathing again. Hargreve returned to the desk and pushed the intercom button. "Claire, get me Hilton Locke on the phone. And let me know as soon as Cristos comes in."

Mac extended his hand to the director. There was an almost imperceptible tremor in Hargreve's grip. He's more shook up about this than he lets on, Mac thought as he left the office, closing the door behind him.

Claire transferred Locke's call to her boss. "How'd it go?" she asked Mac.

"I've got just over forty-eight hours to prove that the wolves didn't kill Donald."

Claire's expression froze. "You mean they didn't . . . the wolves didn't . . . then who?"

"That's what I have to find out. You know just about everything that goes on around here. We need to talk."

"Sure."

"How 'bout we grab a beer, maybe dinner, after work? In the meantime I'm gonna poke around. Can I get into Stewart's office?"

"It should be open. He was always losing the key, so he just quit locking it." Tears started to well up again and she wiped them away roughly. "Dinner'd be great. Let me meet you."

"How about seven at the Cannery?"

"Fine."

Mac left the building without the foggiest idea of how to begin.

•　　•　　•

"Mr. Hargreve, Mr. Cristos just arrived in his office. Do you want me to page him?" Claire's voice asked over the intercom.

"No, I'll take care of it. Thank you."

Hargreve hurried down the hall to the big office at the other end of the building. Cristos was just removing his jacket when Hargreve strode into the room and shut the door.

"Where the hell have you been?" Hargreve demanded.

"You missed me. I'm touched."

"Cut the shit, Cristos, you don't know all that happened here last night. I've been trying to reach you."

"You really should do something about your nerves, Ed."

Hargreve took the second note out of his jacket pocket and threw it at Cristos. It fluttered down onto the desk.

"*That* was waiting for me in my office, before I went down to talk to the police about Stewart."

Cristos sat down and slowly read the message. "So, our mysterious pen pal has surfaced again."

"No damn kidding," Hargreve said, collapsing into a chair.

" 'The lion's share is mine.' Still doesn't tell us much. Share of what?"

"Are you drunk? He knows. Maybe everything. He wants in."

"Maybe."

"Maybe!" Hargreve's voice rose an octave. "There've been two deaths and two notes. You need a map? This"—pointing at the note—"is about as subtle as a wrecking ball."

Cristos pulled out a cigarette, lit it, and took a long drag. "Could be. But it doesn't say enough." He exhaled. "We're sorta stuck till our mystery man makes himself a little clearer."

Hargreve practically leaped from the chair. "Yeah, right, Cristos. The police aren't going to knock on your door when they start looking for someone with a motive. I'm the one here with my pants down. We've got to do something."

"We will. As soon as we know what it is he wants. This is one big cat-and-mouse game, with some very good mental terrorism. And I'd say from the looks of you, it's working."

Cristos was cool, in perfect control, and Hargreve hated him.

Cristos played everything a little too well. And maybe, if he's right, just maybe, I'm talking to the cat, Hargreve thought.

Hargreve took a cold, calculating appraisal of the man behind the desk, turned silently, and left the room.

•　　•　　•

Mac headed off toward Stewart's office, cutting back through the underground tunnel. A few more of the overhead light bulbs had burned out, making it a dim and eerie passageway. A zebra skull gaped from a niche in the smooth concrete walls. Mac picked his way past hayforks, garden hoses, and cobwebs.

He surfaced from the tunnel and walked down the narrow hallway to the office door labeled "General Manager." Looking quickly around, he stepped inside, shutting the door behind him.

Stewart's office wasn't much bigger than his own, but it was better organized. Folders stood neatly arranged in trays. A pencil cup held an assortment of various colored pens. A row of filing cabinets filled one wall. Mac tried a couple and found them locked. Stewart's khaki zoo jacket hung waiting on a brass clothes tree.

The office was just what Mac had expected. Stewart was a man whose entire life had been neat and orderly. Mac stepped behind the desk and sat down. Even the desk blotter was clean. Mac pulled open a couple of drawers full of neatly stacked forms and papers.

He turned to Stewart's appointment calendar. Two weeks back was a note to meet Mac on his first day. He flipped hastily ahead to the next few days. Various committee meetings were penciled in. Mac turned forward one day. At 10:00 A.M. Stewart had written the name "Rorke." Nothing else was noted until the entry for last night's Development Committee. Mac took a last look around the office, stood, and started to leave when a piece of gray newsprint caught his eye.

Tucked into the back of the calendar was a New York news-paper clipping dated January 18 of that year. Mac quickly scanned the article, which reported an investigation of a New Jersey teamsters' union for employee pension fraud. According to the paper, a Newark bank officer had also been implicated in the scheme. The union's leaders were denying any involve-ment in the scandal and insisted any wrongdoers would be fully prosecuted.

Mac read the article a second time. Why would Stewart be interested in a New Jersey teamsters' union? Mac folded the clipping and slipped it carefully into his wallet, then he jotted down the name of Rorke and added that to his wallet. Mac let himself out of Stewart's office, careful that no one saw him.

•   •   •

Mac entered the ape house as the keeper was reaching for the walkie-talkie. "I was just going to page you. It's Molly. She's acting weird this morning."

Mac set his treatment bag down. "In labor?"

"No, I don't think so. It's more like upset, nervous. Pacing around. Wouldn't eat her frappe this morning." The keeper held up an untouched container of the high-nutrition drink the apes received each morning. It was usually one of Molly's favorites.

Mac headed for the gorilla's enclosure with the keeper at his heels. Molly was pacing back and forth along the front of her twenty-by-fifteen–foot birthing pen. Her bedding looked as if it had exploded. She was definitely not her usual self.

Mac watched as the big ape fidgeted with an unopened ba-nana. She finally threw it against the wall, where it hit with a dull thud.

"Anything unusual happen today?" Mac asked.

"Nothing. She was like this when I came on this morning. I

don't know what happened. She was fine when we left last night."

Mac glanced over at the video camera aimed at Molly. From its angle it could scan every move within the enclosure.

"I don't think she's sick or in pain. More like uptight. Spooked. I'll check the tape and let you know if there's anything on it. Let's put her out with her group. Maybe it'll take her mind off whatever's bugging her."

Mac reset the camera for that night's vigil and walked over to the monitoring room. Esther, the docent director, was just packing up her things.

"You on last night, Esther?"

The woman nodded. "I'll be on for the next few nights, too." She handed Mac the record sheet. "Had a busy night last night. Molly had insomnia. And Sienna was really bent out of shape . . . must have been all those police tramping around." She looked down at the table, running her thumbnail down a crack in the wood. "I heard about Donald. I just can't believe it. Those wolves worshiped him."

Mac sighed. "I know. I just never would have figured it. But that shouldn't have upset Molly. I need to see her tape."

As Esther left, he set up the tape and fast-forwarded through the beginning. At around 7:00 P.M. nothing was out of the ordinary. Molly was curled up, sleeping soundly.

Mac ran the tape ahead. Just before 7:30, Molly suddenly woke. She rushed forward to the far end of her enclosure, barking at something off camera, shoulder slamming the bars, and watching it move past her. The camera showed her lips pursed tightly, her body posed high on rigid knuckles.

Suddenly the picture was interrupted by two blurred white objects passing very close to the lens. Mac stopped the tape and rewound it. Two white objects went by one at a time, a split second between them.

Mac rewound the tape again and put it into slow motion as

the first object appeared full screen. He advanced the tape frame by frame. As the first one left and the second appeared, the vet saw the word "Nike" spelled across the back of a large white sneaker.

Mac picked up his walkie-talkie and called the security chief. "O'Malley, would you have Jeff Vincent see me as soon as he comes on?"

"Sure, Doc. There a problem?"

"No, no problem. Just want to talk over something with him. No big deal. Have him page me." There was no point in getting the kid into more trouble. He was already on Hargreve's list. No one was supposed to go into the ape house at night. It disturbed the gorillas. But Jeff was new and probably didn't know better.

"Oh, Doc, I just got a page from the arachnid department about some spiders that escaped this morning."

"What kind?"

"Don't know. I'm on my way there now. Guess they discovered them missing when they came on duty."

"Thanks, Chief, I'll keep an eye out." Mac signed off.

Mac put Molly's tape back on the rack, feeling a whole lot better, and headed for the cafeteria. It was empty except for Decker, sitting at a far booth. Mac collected two doughnuts and a coffee with cream and walked over to where the keeper was sitting.

"Mind if I join you?"

Decker shrugged. Mac slid in opposite him.

Mac took a swig of coffee and a huge bite of doughnut. "One hell of a night," he said with his mouth full.

Decker nodded. "Sorry I wasn't here to help. Jeff Vincent called while I was at the Chief's house last night."

"O'Malley's house?"

Decker nodded. "Poker. Every Tuesday night at O'Malley's. Boy, I shoulda gone home last night." The keeper pulled a bank receipt out of his wallet, which was lying on the table. He stared at the slip in disgust. "Lost all of it, plus what I already had on me. Shitty luck." He tossed the slip down on the table. Mac could see the printed $200.00 amount withdrawn last night at 7:32 P.M.

"Pretty rich game. Those stakes are way out of my league," Mac said.

"Mine too, apparently." Decker stuffed the paper back into his wallet. "Course Joe Waters lost more than that. A couple of the guys did. You should have seen O'Malley. He was winning when he had to leave."

"How many guys played?" Mac asked casually.

"Countin' me, six, no seven, to start. Me, some guy named Bob, and the guards, all 'cept Jeff. O'Malley left to come back here. Then two guys went home around midnight after their wives called pissed. The five of us played till, I don't know, three, four this morning." Decker rubbed his eyes. "I'm getting too old for all-nighters."

"You played six hours?"

"Eight. Game started at six o'clock." Decker grinned and leaned back in the booth. "I was in this game once, in Tanzania. Real high octane. Couple of Arabs flew in on their private jets." Decker leaned forward, hands adding to the story. "Game went for thirty-six hours. No breaks, except for pit stops. Some heavy cash changed hands that game, I'll tell ya. Those 'Rabs weren't what you'd call real good losers. Thought I'd never get out in one piece." Decker's eyes had lit up from the back. Mac had never seen him so animated.

"When I was in 'Nam we used to have a game to break the boredom. Between actions. You in 'Nam?" Mac asked.

Decker glanced away. "Been lots of places. Joined the service to see the world. Didn't you?"

Mac laughed. Decker stood up, stuffed his wallet back into his pants pocket, and sauntered out the door.

Mac took the last bite of doughnut and reviewed who had been on the grounds last night. Jeff Vincent was on guard duty. Twelve Development Committee members were in a meeting. Nat Watermann was finishing up his work. The docent director was at her monitoring post. Not exactly a list of hard-core criminals.

Mac's walkie-talkie chirped from its clip on his belt. Mac picked up the cafeteria's phone and dialed the front desk. Amelia Ball, the zoo's eighty-five-year-old wealthy benefactress, had called and needed to see him.

One of the unwritten responsibilities of his position was caring for the medical needs of Ms. Ball's nineteen cats. While he didn't mind the veterinary care, he did mind having to sit through the obligatory tea and chat that each visit seemed to require. This was the third visit to the Ball estate in two weeks. He sighed, picked up his treatment bag, and headed for the parking lot.

Mac's battered and faded 1966 Land-Rover stood in its designated spot. His California friends had kidded him about driving a safari vehicle in the middle of New England, but Mac had fallen in love with the Rover just before he had gone east. The drive across country had been a test of his determination and kidneys, but the old truck had managed to grind itself to Boston in one piece.

The Rover clattered past the estate's uniformed security guard and coughed to a stop in the circular driveway. A stiffly pressed butler opened the heavily carved front door a split second after the bell rang.

The sitting room was exactly as it had been on Mac's last visit. In fact, it looked as if nothing had changed in years. Only the positions of the assortment of cats had moved.

Mac scooted one hefty tabby over so he could sit down on the sofa. He opened his treatment bag and took out his stethoscope. A movement at the doorway caught his eye.

Amelia Ball paused for a second before she glided into the room. Even at her age, the woman moved with an air of authority. She had made her fortune herself, in a man's world, without benefit of husband or family, and was proud of it. Even snow-white hair did nothing to diminish her impact. She must have been high-volt electric in her younger days, Mac thought. In fact, he had been told she still wielded a considerable amount of influence in the small New England community.

"Thank you for coming, Dr. MacIntire."

"My pleasure. Is one of the cats ill?"

"Oh, yes, poor Geselda. She hasn't eaten in days. I'm quite concerned. Let me see now, where is she?" Ms. Ball scanned the cats littered around the room. It seemed every horizontal surface was breathing. "Oh, dear, she must have heard me call you. Joseph will find her."

Mac suppressed a smile as the old woman called to her butler, who moments later came in carrying the feline at arm's length.

Geselda was even less happy. She loudly voiced her protests as Mac gathered the ample armful. He placed her in his lap and put on the stethoscope one-handed. It didn't look like Geselda had suffered from the missed calories.

While Mac wrestled with his patient, Joseph returned with a silver tea service, poured two cups, and quietly retired. Ms. Ball chattered on about her animals, who were obviously the center of her life. Mac muttered appropriate noises as he struggled to examine the cat. A nasty scratch appeared on his wrist as Geselda stubbornly defied his attempts. Mac gritted his teeth.

"Such a shame. Really quite tragic. And such a lovely girl, too," Ms. Ball chattered. "Almost Shakespearian in its irony, don't you think? First H. L., then Joanne."

"I'm sorry, Ms. Ball, what were you saying?" Mac asked, exasperated. Geselda responded with a deep-throated hiss.

"That's quite all right, Geselda can be quite wayward. You naughty girl, be nice for the doctor," Ms. Ball chided. "I was speaking of H. L. Hargreve and Joanne Nordstrom. I have known the Hargreve family for years. In fact"—she smoothed down an imagined stray hair—"H. L.'s father, Nelson, was a beau of mine once. And H. L. I've known since before he was born. A delightful man. A credit to the Hargreve name."

Mac nodded, released the indignant Geselda with a sigh of relief, and shoved the stethoscope back into the bag.

"Please, Dr. MacIntire, have your tea before it gets cold. Tea must be hot to be properly enjoyed."

Mac picked up the fragile bone china teacup in hands that suddenly felt like lacrosse sticks. Another cat, the size of a sumo wrestler, meandered nonchalantly across his lap. Mac juggled the cup and saucer as the cat's tail trailed defiantly across his nose.

"You must know Ed Hargreve very well then," Mac said politely.

Ms. Ball sniffed audibly. "That one. Such a problem. Poor H. L. was quite beside himself, you know. Always having to bail his son out of one mess after the other. He was quite the embarrassment. I'm certain the only joy H. L. had these past few years was his work at the zoo and, of course, Joanne."

Mac choked on a swallow of the bitter tea. "Nordstrom?"

"Of course. They had been, well, friendly, for a number of years."

Mac was thunderstruck.

"It wasn't common knowledge. Wouldn't have been proper. I know,"—the old woman lowered her voice—"because my maid's sister, June, was H. L.'s maid. The help always know about these things.

"Actually, winter-spring relationships are quite romantic, don't you think, Dr. MacIntire?" She looked at him out of the corner of her eye as she delicately sipped her tea.

He felt himself starting to blush. Geselda had missed a meal about as much as he had. Ms. Ball was certainly full of surprises.

"Yes, ah, quite tragic. H. L. will certainly be missed," Mac said. "I think Geselda is fine. Most likely a fur ball. If she still is not eating in a couple of days, call me. Meanwhile a little corn oil in her food will help." Mac hurriedly stood up. "Thank you for the tea, Ms. Ball."

She smiled graciously and extended a warm, dainty hand, her eyes sparkling mischievously. Joseph appeared from no-where to usher him to the door.

•　　•　　•

Back in his office Mac found a message from Kirby waiting for him. Mac dialed the police station, unclipped his radio and set it on the desk, and paced back and forth at the end of the phone cord, waiting.

"Detective Kirby, Rockland Police Station. You're being recorded."

"This is MacIntire."

"So what's the deal with the wolves?"

"Hargreve agreed. I have two days. If I can't come up with anything, then I put them down Thursday at five P.M. Okay?"

"I think you're barking up the wrong tree"—Kirby started to laugh—"but that's your problem."

"Has the medical examiner fixed the time of death?"

There was a short pause as Mac heard papers rustling around. "Yeah, seven-thirty P.M. Give or take."

"Like how much?"

"Jesus, MacIntire, what am I, psychic? Estimates of death vary. In this case, oh, an hour. Somewhere between seven-thirty and eight-thirty. You found the body a little after nine, right? That help ya, Sherlock?"

It was clear Kirby enjoyed confrontations. They probably made his job more interesting.

"We ran a criminal records check on all the zoo employees.

Looks like everyone's been good little boys and girls," Kirby said.

"What'd the lab say about the tape being cut on that snake box?"

"The findings were inconclusive. The boys couldn't rule it out one way or the other."

"What about fingerprints?"

"It was clean. 'Cept for the victim's prints and one other's."

"Who?"

"Yours." Kirby let that sink in.

"I told you I picked up the box. That's how I noticed the tape on the bottom was cut."

"Uh-huh. Think I'm gonna keep an eye on you, MacIntire."

Mac couldn't tell if he was kidding. "Why, thank you, Detective. And I'll be certain to keep you posted on my progress," he said and hung up.

Mac sat down at his desk, opened a couple of drawers looking for a pen, and heard a familiar squeaking coming down the hall. Seconds later a hand rapped on the frosted glass as Jeff Vincent's head appeared at the door.

"O'Malley said you wanted to see me?"

Mac waved him in. "Do me a favor. I've got a pregnant gorilla in the ape house who's a little jumpy. She didn't enjoy your visit last night. All you need to do is check the exterior of the ape building and the boiler system, not inside."

Jeff scuffed an oversized Nike. "Geez, thought I had to go inside all the buildings."

"All except the apes. No harm done. About what time were you there?"

"I don't know. Shoulda been seven-thirty or so. Maybe a little before. I can check the log."

"No, that's okay, I just wanted to note it on Molly's records."

"Thanks for not telling O'Malley. I owe you one. Hargreve's

already complained about the sneakers. I'm trying to get up the money for some boots." Jeff waved as he ambled out of the office, his sneakers obvious on the linoleum floor.

Mac pulled open the bottom desk drawer and took out the top medical chart, opened the front cover, and stuck a pen behind his ear. He leaned back into his favorite position and propped his feet up on the desk. Back to the salt mines.

He was halfway through the second chart when he felt a slight shift of his pants leg, an almost imperceptible movement. He changed his position, preoccupied with the chart, but then the fabric moved against him again, this time just above the ankle bone.

Mac glanced casually downward to see a deadly two-inch Australian funnel-web spider making its deliberate way toward the bare skin at the top of his sock. Mac sucked in his breath. Once disturbed, these spiders were known to attack anything, regardless of size.

A funnel-web's bite is lethal to children in less than two hours and to adults in twelve. It is a gruesome way to die, with drenching perspiration, frothing at the mouth, muscle spasms, asphyxia, and eventual heart failure. When he had been an exchange student in Sydney, Mac had seen a twenty-year-old construction worker die from a bite. Even worse, only an experimental antidote existed—and that was at least a day away by plane.

Sweat broke out across his body and began to roll down between his shoulder blades. Slowly he reached down toward the open drawer to grab something to flick off the arachnid. His breath came short and quick, every muscle fiber screaming at him to run.

There was no mistaking this aggressive spider. The front body and legs were a smooth and high-gloss jet black. Sparse reddish-brown short hair randomly covered the rear and underbelly, barely concealing twin spurs on the male's rear legs. This spider's body was lifted, its fangs raised and forward, ready, in strike position.

As Mac's hand reached the drawer, another movement caught his eye. From the open drawer came the rapid, jerky crawl of more funnel-webs. The desk was alive with death.

His heart pounding, Mac soccer-kicked his leg, launching the spider into midair, and threw himself backward off the chair. The chart hung overhead, suspended, then fell heavily onto the desk, sending an empty coffee cup flying. With a crash, Mac landed on the floor, flat on his back. The air rushed from his lungs with a grunt as pain seared through his right shoulder.

Watermann, passing by, stuck his head in the door. "You miss the chair or something?"

Mac scrambled to his feet, bolted for the hallway, shoved Watermann out of the way, and slammed the door behind him. "Funnel-webs. God, they're everywhere," he gasped. "Get Spiderman. Now."

Watermann ran for the nearest walkie-talkie. Mac held onto the knob as if he expected the spiders to wrench open the door. He quickly checked himself for more. Starting to shake, he leaned against the wall and vomited.

Chapter 5

Mac watched apprehensively as George "Spiderman" Anderson, the arachnid keeper, deftly snared the spiders one at a time.

"Guess these guys like your taste in furniture," the keeper said. "I've been looking for them all morning. Someone didn't put the lid on right."

Mac just nodded, unable to answer, his stomach still queasy. This was no coincidence. The chance of five escaped, poisonous spiders all camping out in his battered desk was less than likely. It was a message, loud and clear. A deadly message to back off. But from whom?

Unable to bring himself to sit back down at his desk, Mac left for the administration building. Finding an empty meeting room, he phoned Kirby.

"So what'd you expect? The whole damn place is a disaster waiting to happen," Kirby said.

"Wait a minute, five poisonous spiders don't just walk out of their container and all end up in my desk. Somebody put them there."

"You asking for police protection? No problem, I'll send over a black-and-white with some Raid, how's that?"

"I'm trying to tell you that none of this was an accident. Joanne Nordstrom's death wasn't an accident, not with the refrigerator going out and the snake box tampered with. Now lethal spiders just happen to get loose and end up in my office. And I know for a fact the wolves didn't kill Stewart."

"It's a jungle out there."

"Well, while you're killing yourself with comedy, a real killer's working overtime out here. And I don't appreciate—"

"Take it easy, take it easy. You're a touchy bastard. Admit it, MacIntire, you're in way over your head. But I'll give you a break. Seems your manager buddy hired a PI right before he died. The investigator called me when he heard about his client. He's an ex-cop, retired early with a bad back. A straight shooter, name of Rorke. He's in the phone book. Tell him I sent you."

Mac recognized Rorke's name from Stewart's appointment book. "What'd Stewart hire him for?"

"Something about a union in New Jersey."

"Thanks, Kirby."

"Don't thank me, I just want you off my back. By the way, Junior Birdman, the wolf area was also clean. Just Stewart's prints, the keeper's—Watermann—and, of course, yours."

"The killer must have used gloves."

"Didn't know wolves wore 'em. Clock's ticking, MacIntire," Kirby said and hung up.

Mac dialed the number listed for Rorke Investigations and set up a meeting at a nearby restaurant with the male voice that answered. It felt like something out of a low-budget movie. Fifteen minutes later he headed out in the Rover.

• • •

Rorke didn't fit his voice. In fact, nothing about him was what Mac had expected. This was no Mickey Spillane. Just a guy with a bad back.

"I need some background information on a couple of people."

"Why?" Rorke eyed him carefully. He shifted his weight slightly on the diner's fake leather seat.

"I think someone is trying to kill me."

Rorke took a gulp of vanilla frappe. So much for the whiskey-sodden private-eye mystique.

"You that important?" Rorke asked.

"To me, yes," Mac said. "I've been poking around at the zoo and somebody doesn't like it. Maybe the same person who didn't like Stewart."

"Thought that was wolves," Rorke said as he changed his position in the chair again and winced.

"Why did Stewart hire you?"

The PI shrugged. "Let's just say I was supposed to investigate something out of state."

Mac fished the news clipping out of his wallet and handed it to Rorke. "This kind of something? I found it in Stewart's office."

Rorke read it over. "Maybe. So who do you want me to check out?"

"How about we start with this clipping. Find out what it's all about. Then check out Edward Hargreve. And his buddy there, Alex Cristos."

"You want routine stuff or dirt?"

"Dirt."

Rorke wrote the names in a small notebook like Kirby's and added Mac's phone numbers at work and at home.

"You known Kirby long?" Mac asked.

Rorke flipped the notebook shut and tucked it into his jacket pocket. "Twenty years on the force."

"He got an attitude problem? Or just a thing against vets?"

Rorke shrugged. "Probably not you. More like his wife. She's a bitch on wheels. He's hardly home, you know, comes in early, stays late. I think Kirby would divorce her if he could afford it. Her main thing is animals, has a house full of strays. So anything she loves, he hates. Just the usual marital warfare," he said, finishing off the frappe in one mouthful. He stood up. "I'll get back to you."

"Don't take too long. You might be short another client." Mac watched the crooked back walk gingerly out of the diner.

•　　•　　•

Hargreve and Cristos studied each other across the wooden expanse of desk.

"This is getting out of hand. We need to back off until things cool down and we find out how much he knows," Hargreve said.

"I keep telling you, relax. Nobody knows anything. . . . They can't," Cristos replied and casually settled back into one of the leather high-backs. He crossed one custom shoe over his knee and took out the ever-present pack of cigarettes.

"How do you know for sure? Could be that second guy. Maybe he's figured it out." Hargreve stood and started pacing back and forth. "Maybe the first hit man talked before he died. Then the second killer'd know about the ambush, you know, about us."

"You've been watching too many movies," Cristos said. "The first hit man never knew who hired him. *We* don't even know who *he* was. All he had to do was arrange 'an accident' for H. L. And all the second hit man had to do was kill the first. Easy. All arranged, anonymous, real neat. The second guy sent H. L.'s ring just like we planned, when it was done." Cristos smiled. There wasn't any humor in his expression.

Hargreve looked down at his father's twenty-four-carat gold, two-carat diamond ring, which sparkled on the ring finger of his right hand. He sat down heavily in the executive chair. The ring felt unusually tight.

"My family knows how to arrange these matters. That is their business. There isn't anyone, alive, who would connect us with H. L.'s death," Cristos said, toying with the cigarette.

At the beginning it had all seemed so simple. Cristos had all the connections that had made it possible, antiseptic even. H. L. would have an accident, a common event in volatile Africa. Then he, Edward, would inherit his father's fifty-five million, pay off his debts, and give a sizable cut to Cristos. Of course neither man had figured on the codicil to H. L.'s will.

Hargreve stared up at the oil painting of his father that still hung in the office. He couldn't wait to get rid of it. The knowing look, those eyes, always staring at him. The former director was smirking, still having the last laugh. The taste in Hargreve's mouth turned sour.

"That damn will. He *owed* it to me . . . so he goes and leaves it to the zoo and that bimbo." Hargreve laughed harshly. "My righteous father and a zoo receptionist twenty years his junior. It's a wonder Joanne didn't kill him."

Cristos shrugged. "Yeah, so, it worked out better this way. You as director and me running the audits and the books. We've got H. L.'s money, after all. Locke's in our back pocket and the Board thinks we walk on water. So, what's the problem?" Cristos's mouth formed a smile again, but his eyes still didn't.

"So if it wasn't the second hit man—your guy—who's sending the notes? The first one said he knew what we are up to. Now he wants the lion's share. What's it mean?" Hargreve fidgeted nervously with his cuff link.

"Come on, Hargreve, you're not exactly Mr. Popularity here. Still plenty of bad feelings about your stepping into your father's job, just like that. Locke leveraged you in over some heavy competition," Cristos said, blowing smoke at the ceiling. "So relax, we've got the books so tight they squeak. Nobody could prove anything if they saw us hauling money out in bushel baskets."

"Maybe Locke's figured it out?"

"Locke got the top position at First Security Bank because of you. He got you this job, you gave him the zoo banking business. You think he wants to shake that? Forget it, it's not Locke," Cristos said as he stood to leave.

Hargreve watched as Cristos noiselessly left the office. He was a dangerous man to have for a partner, sort of like swimming with a shark. It either goes along with you, or it has you for lunch.

Hargreve had risked teaming up with the man only because Cristos was such a master at financial sleight-of-hand. He had proved that down in New Jersey. But, more important, Cristos's family had the means to H. L.'s fifty-five million dollars. And, Hargreve had to admit, for that he would have teamed up with anybody.

He moved to the discreetly concealed office bar and poured himself three fingers of Pinch. It burned all the way down and didn't help.

•　　•　　•

Mac caught up to Cristos just as the man was unlocking his office. Mac was running out of time and he needed information. As chief financial officer, Cristos had worked with Stewart as closely as anyone.

"You got a minute?" Mac asked, following Cristos into the office and shutting the door. "I'm beginning to have some serious doubts about the wolves' having killed Stewart. You two worked pretty close. Did he have any enemies that you're aware of?"

"I really didn't know him all that well." Cristos took a drag from an already lit cigarette. "And of course, I only knew him in reference to work. What his personal life was I haven't the foggiest. But enemies? Not that I know of. He and Ed weren't exactly merry bedfellows, but I wouldn't say lethal enemies." He smoothed down the paisley silk tie with one slow, sweeping gesture. "What makes you think the wolves didn't do it?"

"Not think, know. And I can prove it," Mac said, bluffing.

Cristos coughed mid-inhale and abruptly stubbed out the cigarette and looked at him closely. "Oh?"

"This was not how a wolf pack would behave. It's just too neat. This was a professional job, you know?" In the dim office light Mac could have sworn something briefly changed in Cristos's face, like a flare igniting for a nanosecond.

"Okay, so who?"

"Well, there are a few loose ends I have to tie up before I want to say, but it's about to come together. Thanks for your time." Mac stood.

"You'll keep me posted? If there's anything I can do to help, just let me know," Cristos said, extending a cool, dry hand.

As Mac left the room, Cristos reached for the phone.

●   ●   ●

The zoo had just closed for the day. The grounds seemed strangely empty without Stewart. The feisty little manager would have been merrily galloping around, kidding workers, cleaning up odds and ends, practically kissing babies, for God's sake. Just went to prove, once again, the good ones always take the pipe, Mac thought.

He stopped by his office, took a shaving kit from his locker, and removed the day's stubble in the speckled exam-room mirror. For some reason that he didn't want to examine too closely, he was a little nervous about meeting Claire. He pulled on a clean shirt and pair of pants he kept in his office. Looking into the mirror, he combed back his thick, dark hair. Though it wasn't supposed to, it felt like a date. His first evening with Sara flickered across his memory and he slammed the locker door shut a little harder than necessary. He heard the Old Spice bottle topple over inside.

•   •   •

The bartender lowered the lights as Mac and the evening crowd streamed in through the oak double doors and up to the bar. Claire was waiting in one of the restaurant's back booths. Two guys at the bar were checking her out. They turned back to their drinks as Mac slid in beside her.

"I've got a head start," she said, tipping what was left of a gin and tonic.

"Right behind you," he said. He signaled for the waitress, ordered an ale, and then changed his mind to Dewar's with a splash. Today was definitely a day for the hard stuff.

"How's it going?" Claire asked.

"I wish I could say something snappy here, but I'm fresh out. It's not going at all. Murder investigation is uncharted water for me."

"And you such a good swimmer."

"Forgot about the undertow." Kirby was right, he was in over his head. "So, tell me what you know about Hargreve. And Cristos. Hargreve and Stewart didn't seem to see eye to eye."

Claire's laugh was short and curt. "That's being polite. Those two squared off from day one. Ed is not an easy man to like. As for Cristos—" she shrugged—"I don't trust a man who can laugh without smiling."

"Things are just so different now," she continued. "Working for H. L. was a partnership in an adventure. There was enthusiasm, goals. Maybe even a mission in life to help the earth. Ed's just a man doing a job and I don't think he even likes it."

"Then why would he volunteer for the position?"

"Beats me. He's, I don't know, self-serving. He and his father were constantly at each other's throats. Ed acted like everything his father worked for was . . . It's hard to explain, irrelevant.

"Ed's always liked the big time. The fancy cars, the Look, you know? Take H. L.'s ring. Ed wears it like a trophy or something. Really bugs me. H. L. worked his butt off, died, you could say, for that game preserve. The Kenyan government gave the ring to H. L. as a token of appreciation. Now Ed wears it because it's valuable, part of his take from the will." Claire picked up her drink and took a big swallow. "Don't get me wrong, Ed's a good administrator, but he's got no heart."

"What did Ed do before he took over his father's position?"

"Worked for some bank in New Jersey, I think. Upper management level. Heard he had some kind of falling out with the upper-upper brass."

"Hargreve brought Cristos with him from the bank job?"

Claire shook her head. "I don't think so. They met while Ed was working in Newark, but Cristos worked for some other outfit. Ed hired him on here a few weeks after he took over the director's position."

Mac let that sink in. "Is Hargreve married?"

"What woman would have him?"

"How 'bout you?" Mac asked.

"What!"

"Married."

"Oh. Do you think I'd be here if I was?" Claire gave him a long look. "No, I'm not. Are you?"

"Used to be."

"Recycled, huh?" Mac stared at her blankly.

"Recycled . . . you know, divorced. Back in the market."

"I'm a . . ." The word stuck to his tongue, refusing to come out. After five years it still seemed foreign, didn't fit. Widowers were old men in their eighties who played endless loops of golf, when they weren't out sport fishing with their cronies. ". . . A widower."

"Oh, I'm sorry."

Mac took a gulp, the ice cubes clinking loudly. He looked at Claire. There was something comfortable and open about her. And for some reason he wanted, maybe needed, to tell her.

"My wife died five years ago. A ruptured ectopic pregnancy. We were camping up in Washington state. Had hiked in so she could finish up an impact study on this lumber company that was mowing down some virgin forest. We knew she was expecting but figured she was still early." Mac signaled the waitress for another round. "Anyway, we'd been camped a few days. She didn't tell me anything was wrong. She was like that. Five-foot-two and tough as nails. She woke me up in the middle of the night in agony." Mac looked out unseeing past the happy-hour crowd jockeying around at the bar. "Had to carry her out. Went as fast as I could down a logging trail but it still took twelve hours nonstop. She lost consciousness about noon and was in shock by the time we staggered into the nearest hospital. They took her right to the OR."

Mac swirled the ice around in his glass. He could see the blood-stained surgeon walking through the swinging doors as if it were yesterday. "Her fallopian tube had ruptured. They tried everything, a hysterectomy, massive transfusions, everything. They said if I had just gotten her there sooner . . ." Mac choked.

Claire reached over and laid a hand on his arm. He gave her hand a squeeze. She politely excused herself to the ladies' room.

The waitress appeared a few seconds later with another round of drinks. "Your friend said you might need this."

His was gone before Claire returned.

Claire slid back into the booth and looked closely at Mac. "You okay?" she asked.

Mac nodded. "Tell me about Watermann."

"Nat? Grew up here in town. In fact, went to high school with Ed. Someone said they used to be good friends once, but had some kind of falling out."

"Ed Hargreve and Nat Watermann were friends?"

"That's what I heard but I've never even seen them speak to each other."

Mac filed that away. The keeper had been there when both Stewart and Joanne had died. In fact, Watermann had been in the hallway when he had found the spiders. It seemed a little too obvious, even to Mac, but anything was possible. And right now he'd take just about anything.

Mac was about to suggest they order dinner when the bartender flipped on the TV. Shots of the zoo flashed behind the anchorman as he told the gruesome story of Stewart's death, described as an accidental encounter with wolves.

Claire watched silently until the newscaster continued with the national news. "What now?"

Mac could feel the pressure grab him like an overzealous Heimlich maneuver. His free time was up. "I know I promised you dinner, but I need to check on something. Would you mind if I took a rain check?"

Claire looked faintly disappointed. "No, of course not."

At Claire's car, Mac leaned a shoulder against the doorframe. "Sorry about dinner. Maybe if I finish up early I could come by for a nightcap?"

Claire smiled up at him. "I might be able to arrange that."

Her dark eyes were shaded as Mac looked down at her smooth skin, the moist lips. Claire was certainly more than he had expected. She had brains and beauty and compassion, and he resisted the urge to pull her close. He hadn't felt like this in a long, long time.

He leaned over and gave her a light kiss on the cheek. "By the way, thanks for listening. I don't usually pour myself all over the table." He grinned sheepishly.

"I'm glad you did," Claire said. "The wolves, they're really important to you, aren't they?"

Mac hesitated, grappling for words. "Once you've lost something that's irreplaceable, you know exactly how much you're losing. Put the coffeepot on," he said, softly tapping the end of her nose, "I'll be over," and headed for his car. The old Rover grumbled into life.

●　　●　　●

Decker's trailer on the edge of town was dark. The mobile home was surrounded by thick woods on four sides. One narrow, rutted driveway sliced through the thickness to the nearest end. A yellow moon outlined the boxy trailer and a forgotten rusted Chevy parked in the weeds on the side.

Mac had hoped Decker could shed some light on Stewart's death. Of all the zoo employees, Decker had the most field experience. Caring for wild animals in the confines of a zoo was a far cry from facing them in their home turf. Out there instinct and survival were one. If the wolves had killed Stewart, it would have been from those basic forces and Decker would know it.

The woods were completely silent except for an occasional unidentified insect chirping in the thicket. Mac pulled out a crinkled remnant of paper and a pencil and scratched down a note and his home number. He climbed down out of the Rover and picked his way through to the front door.

The grass hadn't been mowed in weeks, if ever, and the result was knee deep. A vague trampled path headed in the right direction. Mac stepped over broken lawn chairs and assorted forgotten household gear. Dark objects Mac couldn't identify stood propped against the trailer.

Mac located the front door, opened the screen, and stuck the note in the crack. He wondered briefly if the keeper would even see it in the dark when he sensed, more than heard, a movement behind him. Cautiously, he turned and peered into the brush. In the moonlight objects were silhouetted against pitch blackness. He started to dismiss the feeling when a large chunk of the darkness began to growl, low and menacingly.

The rumbling, hair-raising snarl came at him suddenly in an explosion of noise and movement. Mac took three quick steps backward, trying to identify the source. He clutched the pencil like a knife and prepared to use it.

Bone-snapping teeth chattered like the report of a machine gun as a huge black dog materialized in front of him. At full stretch the animal was easily as tall as he was. Mac felt adrenaline pump through him as the dog launched itself into the air, going for his face. Mac recoiled, bringing his hands up in defense, and prepared to grab the dog's windpipe.

He waited for the impact, estimating the animal's body would hit him at chest level, bringing him down to the ground. Mac planted his back foot to brace himself and felt it catch on something. As he tried to free it, he stumbled and pitched over backward and to the side. The animal came down within inches, and lunged savagely at him, flecks of hot saliva peppering his face.

A glint of moonlight reflected off the heavy chain that rattled backward from the dog's spiked collar to the trailer's undercarriage. The dog was so close he could read the name "Satan" lovingly engraved on the collar's brass plate. Mac rolled quickly into the weeds.

Reaching down, he freed his foot from the snake snare that had tripped him and threw it at the dog. Satan continued to snap viciously, throwing himself to the end of the straining chain. Satan clearly wanted him for a late-night snack and there was no question the battle-scarred dog was strong enough to deliver it. Scrambling up, Mac retreated hastily to the Rover.

Tired down to his very bone marrow, Mac hauled himself back into the old truck and aimed it down the rutted driveway. He thought about his apartment with the single battered sofa waiting for guests who never came. He knew where he'd rather be.

Chapter 6

Barking came from about knee level on the other side of the door at the sound of Claire's doorbell. Small claws stopped their work abruptly when a female voice spoke.

Claire opened the door and stood aside as Mac stepped through. A compact, dark moving ball of fur made frenzied figure eights around her ankles until she snared it on its next pass. "Eek, calm down," she said to the tangle, "this is Mac, a friend." Small eyes sparkled under a heavy fringe of bangs.

Mac reached out his hand and was greeted by a tentative pink tongue. "Eek?"

Claire laughed—it was a solid, healthy sound. "I was putting my trash into the dumpster a couple of years ago when something moved," she said as she led the way into the apartment. "I thought it was a rat and started screaming, until it started to bark. I don't know who scared the other the most. Anyway, he's been Eek ever since."

The little dog jumped down from her arms and up onto the floral sofa. He had obviously landed the good life. Mac joined Eek on the couch and he climbed into his lap.

"He likes you. That's unusual. Coffee?" Claire asked, heading into the kitchen.

"Extra caffeine, please."

"That bad, huh?"

"Worse." Mac rubbed his chin. There was a slight tremble to his hand and he closed it quickly into a large fist. Somewhere deep down in that emotional muck was anger, raging anger. It was always like this, man against animal, man against nature, man against himself. And man never learning anything. He leaned his head back on the couch and closed his eyes. Eek settled down and sighed, content.

"You look dead on your feet," Claire said as she came into the room, balancing two steaming cups of coffee.

She wore an oversized hot-pink T-shirt, belted at the waist, outlining a distinctly female figure. Long legs disappeared up under the mid-thigh hemline. Dark wavy hair fastened on top of her head revealed a graceful neck and finely chiseled features. Her face was completely free of makeup, and Mac thought she had never looked more beautiful. Like an exotic, vibrant flamingo.

He felt at home here. A new place and person to care about.

He took a gulp of the dark coffee. "So, tell me about you. You know my story," he said.

Claire tucked one foot underneath her as she sat down next to him on the sofa. "Not much to tell, really. Graduated from a women's college here in Boston, married the next month, and was divorced seven years later. Moved into this apartment and have been here ever since. No kids, no alimony, no strings."

"Sounds civilized."

"It never is."

"Right." Mac got up, restless, and walked over to the window, looking out at the harsh lights of the parking lot.

"You okay?" she asked, watching him.

Mac shrugged without turning. "I'm sorry, it's just been a hell of a day. Seems it's like that a lot lately. Frustration levels completely off the chart . . . I thought somehow it'd be different here. That I'd finally be able to make a difference."

His memory drifted back to another time. "I left premed to enlist for Vietnam. Guess I believed in the good guys. Things seemed simple, real clean-cut, you know? I thought it was about a political issue. But it wasn't. Maybe it never is, that's just a convenient excuse for down-and-dirty human nature." Mac propped a shoulder against the window frame. "We act all horrified when man does exactly what the animals do, except, of course, we're more efficient at it. We get to use the fancy stuff—guns, knives, explosives, legal contracts. We mouth how terribly unfortunate it is but, of course, necessary, for whatever reason we justify. The only real difference between us and the animals is that we don't eat our kill."

Claire let out a soft rush of breath. "That's a pretty heavy indictment."

"Well, you tell me, does it really make a difference whether you kill a man with a gun or you kill his life's work with corporate maneuvering? And that's what we do to creatures who *are* capable of fighting back. The really helpless ones, the animals, the environment, the planet, don't stand a chance."

"I was in a zoo once that had a huge mirror right at the front door," Claire said. "It was the very first thing the visitor saw. Over it was a sign that read, YOU ARE LOOKING AT THE WORLD'S MOST DANGEROUS ANIMAL. Pretty accurate description."

Mac stared out the window, silent.

"That's why people like you have to stand up for the things that really count," Claire continued.

"I don't know, maybe it's too late for society. No one cares anymore," Mac said. "Donald Stewart gets killed, for God's sake, and it's nothing more than a minor blip on the big screen of life.

"I've been fighting for ten, no, fifteen years and what good has it done? The power holders lobby for their personal interests, they get political support, and the bulldozers fire up. It's a losing battle." Mac pressed his forehead against the cool window glass. "So why not just lie low and stay lost in all the petty things that can tick away the days."

"Could you?"

"You don't understand," he said, his knuckles white, pushed hard into the window frame. "It makes *me* want to get violent. Isn't that a laugh? Here I want things to improve and, when they don't, all I want to do is go find the nearest AK-47. It's almost like all man can understand is something or someone bigger than he is, someone who can knock him on his backside."

He turned back to the window as a thin, stray cat cautiously stepped out into the lot's pinkish light and dashed across the asphalt to hide under the Rover. A safety zone in its hostile world.

"What scares me is I'm no different," he said softly.

Claire came up behind him and put her arms around his waist, resting her head in the hollow between his shoulder blades. He could smell her faint scent of coconut and feel her warm, gentle curves.

"You've been slugging it out alone for too long, my friend," she whispered, muffled by his shirt.

He turned and pulled her close, burying his face in the soft space between her neck and shoulder. He let himself drink in her warmth. He wanted to stand there motionless forever.

She pulled back from him and looked into his tired dark eyes, as if reading his mind. "You want to stay here tonight?"

"Thank you," he said as he brushed back a strand of her dark hair. "It's late and I'm just not up to it, emotionally or physically. Besides mixing business with pleasure, and all that." He smiled wryly.

"Sometimes," she replied slowly, "for something important, you have to take a risk."

Mac leaned down and gave her a wistful, lingering kiss. Claire could, he knew, make him a happy man.

The tangle of fur followed him down the hallway and whimpered as he let himself out of her apartment.

•   •   •

The alarm clock indicated 5:00 A.M. and Mac was still awake, lying on his back, staring through the receding dimness at the swirled plaster ceiling. He rolled over and punched the pillow into shape for the hundredth time that night. Finally in exasperation he got up and in his shorts padded out to the kitchen to make the coffee.

He thought he heard the first ring of the doorbell, his head buried inside a large box looking for the silverware. He checked his watch on the second. Looking through the peephole, Mac saw Kirby leaning against the iron railing, his coat collar pulled up against the cold morning air.

"Do you know what time it is?" Mac demanded as he wrenched open the door.

"Yeah, time to work," the detective said as he strode into the apartment without being invited.

Mac started for the bedroom. "Wait a second, and I'll put on some pants."

"Take care of this while you're at it," Kirby said, pulling out a tiny gray kitten from inside his raincoat.

The kitten was wet, thin, and only a couple of weeks old. Bleary blue eyes blinked in a head that looked too large for its scrawny body. Kirby pushed it into the vet's hands.

"It's pretty young and I figured you'd know how to take care of it," Kirby said gruffly and turned away.

Mac stood staring in amazement as the kitten mewed weakly. Kirby was the last person he would have guessed would arrive at his door with an animal, needy or otherwise.

"Where the hell did you find him?"

"I stopped some jerk for littering on the way to the precinct this morning. It was still dark and I thought he'd thrown some litter out the window. I gave him a citation and started back to the cruiser when I heard a noise. This is what I found in the bag. The other one didn't make it."

Mac handed the kitten back to the detective. "Here, hold him while I get a heating pad and some formula. He must be half frozen."

"I kept him warm inside my coat."

Mac stared at the detective, amazed again. "You're wrecking your image, Kirby," he said as he rummaged through some boxes.

"A momentary lapse," Kirby growled, collapsed onto the tattered sofa, and slowly appraised the apartment. "Hope you didn't pay the decorator."

With a sound of victory Mac held up the plug end of a heating pad. He emptied the rest of the box's contents into another and lined the bottom with towels. Plugging in the heating pad, he collected the frail kitten from Kirby and nestled it down into the box. Mac's disappearance into the kitchen was followed by the din of clanging pots.

"From the sounds of it, remind me not to eat here," Kirby yelled. "You think he'll make it?"

Mac returned with a small nursing bottle filled with diluted feline replacement milk. "I've always brought home orphaned animals, and this is just what the little guy needs. I think he'll survive."

"Fang." Mac looked at the kitten, which was almost lost in the folds of the bedding. "He'll grow into it," Kirby said defensively.

"Mind if I ask why you brought him here? Why not to your wife?"

"I wouldn't give the broad the satisfaction," Kirby muttered. He stood abruptly and stomped to the door.

"When do you want him back?" Mac asked.

"Oh no. No. Him, I don't need," Kirby said, glancing around again, "but from the looks of it, you do."

The detective turned, paused, and checked his watch. "Thirty-six hours and counting, MacIntire." The door slammed hard behind him.

Mac stared at the door long after Kirby had gone. Reaching down, Mac placed the kitten in his lap, its purring the only sound in the barren apartment.

•　　•　　•

An hour later Mac had dropped Fang off in a private part of the zoo's nursery for some food and tender care. He then headed for the video monitoring department. He sorted through the tapes until he located the one of Sienna's first exercise on the night of Stewart's murder.

Mac inserted the tape into the VCR and watched as the first two hours of the docent watch flashed by in fast-forward. Sienna hobbled about without putting weight on the injured leg. Just after seven o'clock, the wolf settled down in her corner bedding and went to sleep. The tape showed her resting peacefully for the next twenty minutes. Mac was about to skip ahead when suddenly Sienna lifted her head.

Ears forward, eyes riveted, her body went visibly taut. She rose cautiously and lowered her head, ears moving back flat against her angular skull. A small sliver of white teeth appeared as the long red fur at the nape of her neck fanned out. Mac instantly recognized the wolf's classic alarm posture.

Sienna moved to the farthest part of her enclosure and bared her teeth. Mac could almost hear her deep, rumbling warning growl.

Across the video frame appeared two white objects. Two brief, but distinct, white objects separated by a split second of space, moving in the direction of the main wolf enclosure. Mac felt the startle of recognition, his stomach one well-defined knot. Mac quickly checked the docent's log—7:37 P.M.—but nothing was noted. He rewound the tape with a prickly feeling of dread.

The sneakers went by this time in slow motion, their white fabric distinctly familiar. Mac slammed the remote control down onto the tabletop. Jeff Vincent had been on tape at the ape enclosure a few minutes earlier. The medical examiner had estimated Stewart's death for the same time. Mac ran a hand across his sweaty face. But this tape placed Jeff at the wolf enclosure only minutes later. Close enough to have been present when Stewart died.

But why? Why would the young security guard want to kill the general manager? Or, using Kirby's argument, if the wolves had killed Stewart, why hadn't Jeff helped him? The attack would have been aggressive and very noisy. Not exactly something that could be easily missed.

"Hi, Doc, any new orders?"

Mac jumped at the sound of the docent director's voice. Esther stood at the doorway, looking expectant. "Uh, no, no, thanks. I'm going to take Sienna's and Molly's tapes with me. I'm working at home tonight," Mac replied. "Esther, I was just going over Sienna's tape from the other night. There was someone at the wolf enclosure in a pair of white sneakers that you didn't note on the record sheet. How come?"

"Oh, that was just Jeff Vincent, the new guard. He was doing his rounds. I don't usually record the guard's visits," she said, suddenly flustered. "Is something wrong?"

"No, I guess not. It was just such a strange night. Thanks."

The woman nodded, looked relieved, and disappeared.

Mac ran the tape forward to 9:00 P.M. It showed Sienna clearly agitated, pacing back and forth and looking in the direction of the other wolves. At 9:10 P.M. the film showed Mac's work boots stumbling past the camera as he lowered the dividing gate and turned on the floodlights.

Mac slowly rewound the tape and removed it from the VCR, staring at the blank monitor screen. Jeff Vincent was shown on both the wolf tape and on the ape film around the time of Stewart's murder. It wasn't the order his route would have taken him, and only about five minutes apart. He would have had to drive—or run—straight from the ape enclosure to the wolves. His arrival at the wolf compound had to be direct and intentional.

Mac collected the two tapes, put them in his treatment bag, and left the monitoring room. Jeff Vincent had the opportunity, but what was his motive to murder Stewart?

Mac stepped outside into the sunlight and took half a dozen steps down the path toward his office. Something was wrong. Something subtle. Elusive, it wriggled at the very back of his brain, refusing to be ignored.

Mac stopped short. Turning, he raced back to the monitoring room, locked the door, and slammed Sienna's tape back into the machine. He forwarded the tape just up to 7:30 P.M. and watched closely. Rewinding, he watched again, and then a third time.

Across the side of the sneakers at the wolf enclosure were the letters "NB," stitched in thread. New Balance sneakers.

Mac quickly put the gorilla tape into the VCR and fast-forwarded to the same time. There on Molly's tape was a large pair of sneakers with "Nike" printed clearly in blue ink across the top back of the heel.

Two different pairs of sneakers. Mac sat down into the chair with a thud. Someone else had been at the wolf compound the night Stewart died. A murderer.

Chapter 7

Mac snatched up the two tapes and hurried to his office. Closing the door, he set the tapes on the desk and reached for the phone. He was halfway through dialing Kirby's number when he put the phone abruptly back on the hook. Kirby would laugh in his face. Two different pairs of sneakers certainly implied two different people, but hardly proved one was a killer. More important, it didn't prove who was *in* the sneakers. Kirby would want hard evidence. So, for now, until he could give Kirby something solid, Mac needed to play his hand carefully, close to his chest. Mac reached for the walkie-talkie just as Decker knocked, opened the office door, and ambled in.

"Got your note."

"Oh, yeah. And I met loving Fido."

Decker grinned, obviously pleased. "I figured you must have run into Satan. He enjoys visitors."

"I could tell. What is he anyway, besides a liability?"

Decker moved over to the desk and sat down on the edge. "A hybrid. Rottweiler-wolf. Got him while I was in South Africa. They're aggressive, fearless, and can run for miles. Used him for protection when out in the bush. I got sort of attached."

Decker glanced down at the videotapes on the desk and pushed one with his thumbnail. "A little late-night entertainment? Anything interesting?" He picked one up and read the title.

"Just tapes of Molly. Trying to figure out why she's overdue." Mac forced himself to act indifferent.

Decker tossed the tape down as Mac quietly let out his breath. "What'd you want to see me for?"

"Wanted your input on what might have happened with the wolves. Guess I really underestimated them. At first I thought something else had killed Stewart, but now, well, it's clear they did it."

Decker shrugged. "Wolves can get pretty wired, especially the pack leader. Stewart must have challenged him somehow. Big mistake. Wolves you should never completely trust."

"Right, well, thanks, Decker. Sorry to have riled up your dog. I'll remember to call before I come over next time."

Decker strolled to the door. "No phone," he said and disappeared into the hallway.

Mac waited a full sixty-second count and then grabbed the video tapes and shoved them into the desk's bottom drawer. Picking up his treatment bag, he left the office, locked the door, took five steps, changed his mind, went back into the office, and put the tapes in his treatment bag. He left the office again and relocked the door behind him.

•   •   •

The ruddy face of the fifty-five-year-old security chief broke into its Irish grin as Mac stuck his head into O'Malley's closet-sized office.

"Got a minute?" Mac asked.

O'Malley waved him in and Mac quickly checked that no one else was in the outer office. He closed the door and sat down opposite the chief. O'Malley looked at him curiously.

"I need your help and it has to be confidential. It's about the night of Stewart's death."

"Sure. What?"

"Who, exactly, was on the grounds from between, say, six and eight-thirty that night?"

"That's easy, wait a minute." O'Malley disappeared into the outer office and returned with the log sheet. "Let's see, well, Jeff Vincent was the night guard. The members of the Development Committee were here—you need their names?"

Mac shook his head. "No, I saw them personally. Anyone else?"

"You, Stewart, and Esther, the docent director. That's it."

"No one else signed in or out during that time? Is there any way someone could get onto the grounds without coming through the security booth?"

O'Malley shook his head. "Not 'less they're a high jumper. All the entrances are locked and checked on each set of rounds. We've got ten-foot chain-link perimeter fencing with barbed wire at the top—we put that in after a problem with some fraternity kids last year. I guess someone could cut their way in if they had the right tools, but we check the fencing every day on the day shift. Part of our insurance coverage. We haven't found any breaks. Why?"

"This is the confidential part. I don't believe the wolves killed Stewart. I think someone got in here and made it look like the wolves."

O'Malley gave him a cool, steady look, the Irish face becoming slightly more flushed. "You telling me my staff didn't do their job?"

"No, that's not what I'm saying. Now don't go getting all worked up, Chief. I think whoever did this knows the zoo and is clever, real clever. Wasn't Watermann here that night?"

O'Malley nodded. "That's not unusual. A lot of the keepers will stay late to do their paperwork. Course that night Watermann was questioned by the police. We all were." O'Malley glanced down at the time sheet. "Guess he didn't sign out. But that night was pretty crazy. In fact, you didn't either."

"Oh, sorry." Mac rubbed an imaginary spot on his forehead. "What about the security rounds . . . could a gate have been missed? Maybe accidentally left unlocked?"

"The guards have to clock in at certain places on their rounds. All of the buildings and gates are included. Jeff hit every one that night, right on schedule. I already looked into that. So did the police. Anything else, Doc?"

Mac shook his head. That confirmed Jeff couldn't have been at the two different compounds five minutes apart and still be on time with his usual security checks. There had been a second person on the grounds that night, wearing the New Balance sneakers. But who? Mac thanked the chief and left.

•   •   •

Stewart's office door closed silently as Mac eased it into the doorframe. There had to be something he was missing. Something that Stewart knew, or had, or stumbled onto. Something that was important enough for murder.

Mac started with the filing cabinets. He pulled a thin rasping file out of his treatment bag and toyed with the lock. The first one popped out after a few minutes of fiddling. Mac was better at it by the time he had opened the sixth.

The files didn't contain anything of importance. Policy sheets, employee records, time cards, payroll accounts. The usual mountain of management paperwork.

Mac turned to the desk, rechecking in and under every drawer. He turned over the pencil holder. Nothing. The office was stuffy and a thin film of perspiration coated his face as he emptied the pockets of Stewart's jacket. Nothing.

He sat down at the desk and looked slowly around the room. Stewart was compulsively neat and the kind of person who felt he had to do everything himself. If he had had something so valuable it had cost him his life, he would have wanted it close, watchable. So, where would he put it?

The ceiling tiles were cemented in place, the floor unbroken vinyl. Fifteen minutes later Mac was still empty-handed. Worse, he didn't know what he was looking for.

Disgusted, he stood, reached for his treatment bag, and turned for the door, the bag swinging forward. It connected with the desk telephone, lifting the black plastic housing up over the dial. Mac stopped and looked at it more closely.

Taking the file, he loosened the screws holding the cover. The internal mechanisms fell heavily onto the desk, releasing a tightly wedged square of paper from behind the bells.

Mac unfolded the papers and smoothed them out on the desk, revealing three reduced photocopies of an accounts ledger. Two pages covered the zoo's receivables and payables for the last two months. The third page was a copy of the zoo's investment ledger.

Mac quickly scanned the figures. Nothing seemed out of the ordinary. All the accounts balanced and the flow of investments in and out of the account seemed reasonable. Mac shrugged and started to put the papers into his treatment bag, changed his mind, and tucked them back into the telephone. He tightened the screws firmly in place.

Why would Stewart hide financial data inside his desk phone? One could only assume that things were hidden when they were valuable or incriminating. And, using that logic, did Stewart hide it because it was connected to himself or to someone else?

Mac let himself out of the office, not liking some of the questions that were flitting around in his mind.

•　　•　　•

Claire was busy at the typewriter, a transcriber earset on her head. Mac stood and watched her for a few seconds before he stepped into her peripheral vision. She smiled, put up a finger for a second more, finished the sentence, and took off the headset.

"Hey there, handsome. What can I do for you?"

"You grant wishes?"

"Depends."

"I hate to use up a perfectly good wish, but I need to see the boss."

"Oh, how boring." Claire touched the intercom button. "Mr. Hargreve, Dr. MacIntire would like to see you."

Mac walked into the director's office and back into the hot seat.

"So, what have you discovered in your investigations, Doctor?" Hargreve leaned back in his thousand-dollar executive chair.

Mac had planned to tell Hargreve about what he had found but something changed his mind just as he opened his mouth. His instincts were flashing caution. "I have a few clues and am working on a strong lead, but nothing I want to put my name to yet."

"I'm afraid I need something a little more concrete than that. You said yesterday that you had proof. So what exactly do you have?"

Mac knew he was cornered. He'd have to give Hargreve something, a peace token, to keep him happy, yet not tip his whole hand.

"There is one thing. It appears Stewart hired a PI right before he died, and Rorke's agreed to continue his search."

"Search for what?" Hargreve's eyes had suddenly gone wary. Mac sensed it too late.

"Ah, I'm not really sure, about some company in New Jersey. I found a newspaper clipping in Stewart's office."

Hargreve jerked up out of his seat and walked over to the mirrored bar. Mac's instincts went into overload.

"I'd like to see the article."

"I left it in my office, sorry," Mac lied.

Hargreve abruptly returned to his desk and sat down with deliberate care. "This charade has gone on long enough, Dr. MacIntire. We will put this entire mess to bed once and for all. I expect you to devote your time to caring for the animals, not amateur sleuthing. Have I made myself clear?"

"But I still have some time before the deadline."

"You're not listening, Doctor—your investigation is over."

"You mean to tell me that you are going to put the wolves down before I have a chance to prove them innocent!" Mac leapt up and strode over to the desk and leaned over the director. Anger had him in its fiery grip, with all discretion gone.

Hargreve looked at him stonily, a fine smear of sweat on his smoothly shaven upper lip.

"We had a deal, Hargreve, man to man. I'm not going to let you weasel out of this. I have until 5:00 P.M. tomorrow and I intend to use it."

"I could just fire you for insubordination and that would end your investigation."

"And maybe the Board would like to hear about this—our deal, my evidence . . . what Rorke is looking for?" He was firing blind into thin air, but it was the only move he had left. He held his breath, waiting for Hargreve's reaction.

Hargreve pushed back from the desk and said with barely controlled rage, "Dr. MacIntire, understand what I am saying. If you continue with this farce, consider your position here terminated."

Mac got some pleasure slamming the huge office door shut as he spun on his heel and stormed out. He took a deep breath on the other side of Hargreve's door.

"I could hear that from out here!" Claire's face was pale, eyes wide.

Mac nodded, still getting himself under control.

"What are you going to do?"

"How much time do I have?" he asked, grinning.

"You don't get involved, you don't take risks. You just jump off the damn building."

"And set it on fire as I go."

"You're all right, MacIntire," she said. "For a while there you had me worried."

He had heard that before. Mac blew her a kiss as he left the office, promising to see her that night. After all, if he was fired, Claire wasn't business anymore.

●　　●　　●

He had half a doughnut down before the full impact of what had just happened careened in on him like a head-on collision. It got his full attention.

"Ah, shit." He propped his chin in his hand and stared out the window at the herbivore complex. He had just blown the best job he had ever had on some half-baked theory. What if he was wrong and the wolves really had attacked Stewart? Doubt flooded into all the unoccupied corners of his mind. But doubt or no doubt, he was going to have to fight this one down to the finish, to the last standing pawn, until someone yelled checkmate.

And there was one thing he knew, without any shred of doubt—if it was possible for Sara to know what was happening, she was behind him all the way. Cheering wildly. And for the first time, the familiar hollow pain of missing her was comforting.

Leaving the cafeteria, the black treatment bag gripped in his hand, he headed for the wolves' enclosure. Sienna was taking her first few tentative steps on the injured leg as Mac rounded the corner.

He stopped and quietly watched. Just a couple of days ago he would have been thrilled at her improvement. He would have called Stewart to share in the excitement of the victory. Sienna would recover. It was ironic that the very attack that had almost killed her would spare her life. She was the only wolf that could not be implicated in Stewart's death. Her mates, her pack members, would be destroyed, she the lone surviving red wolf. The world's population would then be down to critical levels.

In front of the wolves' glass viewing area a few visitors craned their necks to see what was inside. Mac waited until they had moved past the area and were involved in the eagle exhibit to enter the enclosure. Toka and his family lolled in the shade of two fallen fir trees. Three six-month-old pups romped over and among the tolerant adults.

Mac admired the wolves' family structure again. Experts consider the wolf to have the most highly developed social organization in the animal kingdom. Hunting is a team effort. Immature animals, too young to participate, contribute by guarding the newborns while the others hunt. Mated pairs stay together for years and even the males help in the care of the young. One playful pup grabbed hold of Toka's tail as the alpha male patiently ignored him.

Recent studies had showed that wolves rarely attack even domestic cattle, unless their natural prey is no longer available or they are crowded into too small a territory to support themselves. Starvation or rabies is almost always responsible for wolves encroaching into man's territory.

So, as usual, it was man who was the aggressor, Mac thought. Yet the fear of wolves as savage killers persisted from out of the medieval ages. That fear alone would be their death sentence, if this ever went to court.

Mac watched as two adolescent males wrestled, looking like two German shepherd pups romping in a suburban backyard. These wolves were neither rabid nor starved. What could have happened with Stewart? Even if Toka had turned on the general manager, it should have been possible to fend him off long enough to get over the fencing to safety.

Why didn't Stewart throw the window cleaning fluid at him or even use the squeegee as a weapon? Stewart's body had looked as if he had still been washing the window. Hardly the position Mac would have expected if attacked by the pack. Nothing added up. And now the videotape showed someone in New Balance sneakers at the scene. But who?

Mac jotted down a note about Sienna's improvement in her medical chart and placed it back in the rack. The afternoon sun was beginning to dip down below tree level and his watch showed four-thirty. Another half an hour and the zoo would close. He had only twenty-four hours left.

•   •   •

There was something about the way the key turned in his office door lock that made him pause. He nudged it open and cautiously peered inside.

The filing cabinets were just as he had left them, the desk drawers still closed, his locker undisturbed. Medical charts lay stacked as before, more or less everywhere. Mac could see through into the exam room. It was the same. But there was something different about the office suite. An almost imperceptible change.

He froze and scanned the room, object by object. The desk chair was swiveled in the wrong direction. His jacket hung on a different hook. The coffee mug sat backward to the left. But Mac was right-handed. He reached for his walkie-talkie. He had learned a long time ago it was the details that mattered.

"Three-four-three-four. Code Seven R. Three-four-eight-one. Over."

The guard booth responded immediately to the break-and-entry call. It would be only minutes before the security team arrived. While he waited for O'Malley, Mac walked around the office noting the subtle changes. The drugs in the cabinet were shuffled but nothing seemed to be missing. His exam instruments and medical supplies were repositioned but there. It was as if the intruder had methodically sorted through the rooms, looking for something specific.

O'Malley arrived within three minutes. "Anything missing?"

"Nothing I can see. Just rearranged. I'm pretty sure all the meds are here, but I'll do a count."

"Keep any money in here?"

"I don't have money anywhere."

"You obviously had something they were looking for. I'll ask if anyone saw anything." O'Malley disappeared, walkie-talkie in hand.

What did Mac have that someone might want badly enough to risk searching his office in mid-afternoon? He didn't own anything of value. He didn't even have anything of value that anyone else owned.

Mac stopped short. Except for the newspaper clipping. And the only person who knew he had the clipping was Edward Hargreve. Mac didn't like the feeling that was brewing in the pit of his stomach.

The phone jangled loudly from its spot on the office desk. Mac reached for the receiver.

"MacIntire? Rorke. I think I got something for ya."

"What?" Mac pulled the chair around and sat down just as Watermann and Decker stepped into the office. Watermann whistled a low, unidentifiable tune as he wandered about the room. Decker draped a beefy arm over a filing cabinet and looked at Mac expectantly.

Mac turned slightly in the chair and lowered his voice. "Maybe I could get back to you?"

"Can't. I'm at the airport and the flight's leaving. Going to Jersey to check it out."

"New Jersey! What we talked about?"

"A mind blower, if I'm right. I'll call you as soon as I'm sure. But better watch yourself." The phone went dead as Rorke hung up.

Mac turned and put the receiver back. Watermann quit mid-note.

"O'Malley said someone had reorganized your office, but I was expecting something a little more impressive," Watermann kidded.

"Everyone's a comedian," Mac replied.

It had been a long day, a long couple of days, and Mac wasn't any closer to finding out who killed Stewart. Even if Rorke found something useful, it might be too late. At 5:00 P.M. tomorrow the wolves would be executed.

The three men walked out into the early September evening.

"Wanta join me for a beer?" Decker asked.

Mac and Watermann both declined, claiming other things to do. The two keepers headed off in the direction of the security booth and Mac to the nursery.

Fang was sound asleep in a tight gray ball when Mac picked him up. He watched the kitten's breathing increase as it became aware of his presence. A soft blue appeared between groggy slits, widening to full round orbs.

"Hey, fella, I think you've put on some weight since this morning."

The little kitten yawned and stretched. A faint rumbling came from the handful as he stroked the kitten's head.

"Looks like we've both been thrown out, huh, guy?" The purring got louder. "I'll take you home tomorrow. When I'm unemployed." He put the kitten back into the bed, left the nursery, and went back to his office.

There was no point putting it off any longer. He dialed Kirby's number and the detective answered on the second ring.

"So, Joe Friday, how's it going? Have anything we can take to court?"

Mac hesitated. "I'm not sure. I found something on my videotapes from the night of Stewart's murder that I think you should see. It may not be enough, but there's something that proves someone, other than Stewart, was at the wolf enclosure near the time of the murder."

"Like what?"

"Sneakers."

Kirby made a noise close to a snort. "Sneakers?"

"Kirby, hear me out. The videotape at the ape house shows the security guard in Nike sneakers just before seven-thirty. The wolf tape shows someone in New Balance sneakers at that enclosure a few minutes later. If he wasn't a murderer, then at least that person should have heard the commotion. Stewart would have certainly yelled for help if he were being attacked. It's not exactly something you take quietly."

"So who's in the New Balance ones?"

"I don't know." Mac paused. "But I mentioned I had that newspaper clipping about the New Jersey union in my office to Hargreve this morning—the one Stewart had Rorke following up—and my office was broken into this afternoon. Nothing missing, but like someone was looking for something."

"Hargreve! Your director?" Kirby was laughing so hard he was gasping. "Your exec went to your office when no one was looking and searched through your office for a newspaper clipping about some union pension fund?" Kirby dissolved back into laughter. "That's it?"

"That's my story."

"What does that have to do with a pair of sneakers? Listen, MacIntire, a word of advice, don't quit your day job."

"Too late."

"What?"

"Never mind." Mac had to admit it sounded pretty weak even to him. Hargreve could hardly have searched the office himself and, even if he had hired someone, why would he care about a union problem? And what did he have to do with a pair of sneakers? Hargreve was probably wearing his usual leather wing tips the night Stewart died. Mac felt himself starting to squirm. He was glad Kirby wasn't there in person. "Okay, so don't bother."

"No, I'll take a look at it. Leave the tapes at the security booth. I'll send a car over for them. See you tomorrow at five sharp. Where do you want me to meet you?"

Guilt hit Mac at gut level like a steel ice pick. He had let the wolves down. Because of him they would die. He wanted to rip the phone out of the wall and grind it into pulp with his bare hands. "At the wolf enclosure," he said softly.

"And the weapon of choice?"

"Listen, you—"

"Sorry," Kirby said. "The lab results came back on the blood found on that big male wolf. It wasn't human. It was wolf blood. Guess Stewart tried to fight back, after all. Thought you'd like to know."

Mac thanked him and slowly put the phone back. It rang again before he could lift his hand.

"Mac?" Claire's voice came over the line. "Amelia Ball just called. She wants to see you as soon as possible. No emergency, but something business."

Mac grinned.

•　　•　　•

Fifteen minutes later the Rover rattled up the sweeping driveway to the front door of the manor house. Joseph promptly answered the bell's ring.

Ms. Ball was standing beside a marble table in the foyer, snipping stems from a bunch of fresh flowers. She methodically tended to each one, adding them to a tall German crystal vase.

Her white hair was coiled up in a loose bun on the top of her head, a few strands escaping down her neck. A floral sundress enclosed a still trim figure. From Mac's vantage point at the door, she could have passed for any age within a twenty-year span.

"Dr. MacIntire, thank you for coming. Please come in. I'm just finishing up. There's nothing quite like the emotional boost of fresh flowers." She continued to clip each stem as she talked.

"I received a message you wanted to see me. Is one of the cats ill?"

Her laugh was light and tinkly. "Oh, no. They're fine. Even Geselda. No, I wanted to talk with you about another matter."

Mac waited, puzzled.

"With all that has been going on at the zoo, quite upsetting, really, I thought I'd best have your assistance with this," she said. "In the past I have always felt comfortable with the fiscal management at Rockland Zoo. You know I have made the zoo one of my primary charities?" She paused, seeming to hesitate. "Let's be frank, Dr. MacIntire. I have some concerns about how donations, some of considerable size, are being handled. My donations, specifically."

"Well, I'm sure that Alex Cristos or Ed Hargreve would be happy to discuss this with you. I'm just the veterinarian. I don't get involved with the financial end of things."

"Come now, Dr. MacIntire, you are a sharp man. And experienced in the business of large zoos. I understand you managed quite a healthy budget in your previous position in California." She gave him an appraising look. "Does it strike you that things are not as they should be out at Rockland?"

Mac watched the robin's-egg blue eyes turn from gentle octogenarian to diamond-hard executive. This was Amelia Ball, business financier, in action.

"Well, ah, there has been some discussion about the postponement of the avian project. Donald Stewart had been fighting that decision just before his death."

"Who made that decision?"

"Ed Hargreve. But the Board approved it."

The woman sniffed. "The Board would follow Ed Hargreve off a cliff. Why was the project postponed?"

"Not enough funding."

"Poppycock. That is exactly what I am referring to," she said, putting the scissors down on the table with an abrupt click. She turned and strode into the sitting parlor and gestured him over to a facing settee. "I personally matched the zoo's half-million for that aviary. The totaled million-dollar sum was more than sufficient to fund even the highest contractor's bid obtained for the project."

"I don't remember seeing your donation listed on the last financial statement at the Executive Committee meeting," Mac said.

"When was that?"

"Three days ago."

"I made the donation to Ed Hargreve, personally, a month ago. So, tell me, what happened to my money?"

"Ms. Ball, I'm in no position to discuss this with any kind of accurate knowledge. All the last financial statement showed was a bequeathal from H. L. Hargreve to the zoo for close to fifty-five million dollars."

Ms. Ball leaned back and folded her arms across her waist. She stared into space for a few seconds. "Fifty-five million, invested at the going rate—let's say we're conservative, nothing flashy or risky—would generate in the neighborhood of five million dollars a year in income. Certainly enough to fund multiple aviaries. In fact, that one investment would return close to the zoo's entire annual budget. Couple that with my gift, and the zoo has some significant capital to play with, wouldn't you say?''

"I would think so.''

"Which gets us back to why you are here. I had planned to donate some additional monies to the zoo to be used specifically for the new veterinary suite. Perhaps some needed medical equipment? But I am reluctant to do so if I cannot be sure how the money is being applied.''

"What are you asking, Amelia?''

"Find out what the hell is going on.''

Mac stared, open-mouthed, at the little lady. She was no lightweight. This was one tough customer who'd get to the pearly gates and tell Saint Peter to shape up. And he would.

"I'll do the best I can. But I don't have access to the zoo's financial records. It's all on computer and I don't have clearance for the security code.''

"Like I said, you're a smart man. The accounts are kept on ledger before the finance department inputs them into the computer.'' She stood and extended her dainty hand. She had a grip like a trucker's. "I am not telling you all this lightly, Mac. I have always had a sense for good business and a nose for when it's not.''

He said his farewells and let himself out the front door before Joseph could appear from somewhere inside the cavernous mansion. Mac was deep in thought as he let the Rover roll back down the long gravel driveway.

●   ●   ●

He couldn't quite dismiss it, the disquieting similarity between the newspaper clipping and the thought that flitted back and forth inside his head. The article had been about the embezzlement of a teamsters' union pension fund. Now there seemed to be some errant money at the zoo—or at least unaccounted for. Hardly something such a meticulous man as Cristos would have missed.

Maybe a closer look at Stewart's hidden copy of the accounts ledger would be in order.

•　　　•　　　•

Mac pulled into his parking spot, reached for his black treatment bag on the passenger seat, and was halfway out of the Rover when he heard his name called. Turning, he saw Hilton Locke sprinting across the zoo's parking lot toward him.

"Glad I could catch you. How's it going?" Locke asked. Mac shook his head. He was getting tired of that question.

"The wolves, they're, uh, going down tomorrow?"

"I'm meeting Kirby at closing. Possibly my last official duty on my last day," Mac replied.

Locke looked puzzled. "What do you mean?"

"Hargreve said if I don't quit wasting my time being Dick Tracy I'll be looking for another job. After I put down the wolves, of course." Mac found himself gripping the doorframe and consciously forced himself to let go.

Locke shifted his weight uncomfortably. "It does seem a little extreme to put them down. After all, they are *wild*. Want me to see if I can reason with Ed? Maybe I can get him to back off on your pink slip."

"Sure, if you think he'd listen. I like it here. Might even settle down permanently. Which reminds me, Hilt, I need to set up an investment account with a local bank. The zoo has its account with your bank, First Security? Right?"

Locke stood a little straighter. "Sure does. First Security is a full-service financial institution. I'd be happy to sit down and discuss it with you."

"Great. I would assume that whatever the zoo invests in would be safe, you know, protected? I'm not interested in walking any tightropes. . . ."

"Oh, very safe, Mac. I handle all the zoo's investment activity personally. They prefer CDs, actually. We have a wide range of maturity dates, depending on your needs . . . and the amount you want to invest." Locke's eyes had begun to shine.

"What maturities does the zoo use?"

"Alex Cristos likes short term. Six months to two years at the most. We stagger the maturities so they come due at intervals over a two-year period."

"Guess H. L.'s bequeathal, the fifty-five million, would take some fancy handling. That must be keeping you busy."

"Oh, Cristos insisted we invest in treasury notes with that large a sum. The bank acts as agent for the zoo in all treasuries purchases." Locke was practically dancing.

"Thanks, Hilt, maybe I'll stop by this week and we can talk it over. I have a little money put aside that I'd like to invest. If I'm still employed."

Locke leaned a little closer and lowered his voice. "I'll see what I can do about Ed. I think all of this has just been a little overblown. You were, ah, thinking of investing around how much—"

"Stewart's death has us all shook up," Mac interrupted. "And I would have staked my career on the fact the wolves didn't do it. But you can't be right all the time. Had to be Toka. The only people on the grounds have all been accounted for. I even saw your committee members myself."

"Right. Stewart never showed up and Ed was the only one who left the meeting," Locke said.

Mac could hardly catch his breath. "Hargreve left the meeting?"

"Just for a minute."

"When?"

"Right after it started."

"Seven o'clock, then?" Mac felt the excitement beginning to deflate. Stewart had been killed closer to seven-thirty.

"No, we started late, more like seven-fifteen or seven-twenty," Locke said. "Now wait a minute, you're not thinking Ed . . . ?"

"No, of course not. I just hate to lose those wolves."

Locke looked relieved. "Well, I'll see if I can go to bat for you about the job. We need your skills here, Doc, with or without red wolves. Give me a call when you want to discuss your finances."

Locke handed him his business card, turned and walked over to his dark-gray Olds, got in, and drove off, leaving Watermann's Jeep the only car keeping the Rover company. Mac slowly sat back down in the driver's seat. The sun slipped down into the zoo's lake while Mac stared blankly out through the windshield. The parking lot's automatic lights flipped on, turning the asphalt a muddy brown color.

The zoo had used CDs, but had just switched their money to treasuries. Why hadn't Amelia Ball's donation appeared on the financial statement? Half a million dollars in the zoo's account would certainly have been invested, even if for only a few months.

Mac jumped out of the car, grabbed his flashlight out of his treatment bag, and headed for Stewart's office by way of the security booth. As Mac signed in on the log sheet, he saw Jeff Vincent sitting in O'Malley's swivel chair lacing up his Nikes. Other than the docent watch, Mac was the only person still signed in.

●　　●　　●

Except for a slight musty smell, Stewart's office was just as he had left it. Mac silently closed the door and locked it. Flipping on the desk light, he opened the bottom of the telephone with a dime and took out the ledger photocopies.

Opening the left top file cabinet, he found the folder of the Executive Committee meeting records and a copy of Cristos's last financial statement. Mac sat on the edge of the chair and started with the account entries for the month of H. L.'s death.

An hour and a half later, Mac tossed the pencil down on the desk and rubbed the back of his neck. Rockland had been running in the black even before H. L.'s will had pushed the zoo's bank balance into the stratosphere. Up until that time, Amelia Ball's steady input of capital had made for a healthy cushion, preventing any need for government funding. Locke's CDs had rolled over on schedule, adding to the sizable income from admissions, memberships, and parking.

During this last month, Cristos had had Locke wire the enormous fifty-five-million endowment to the Federal Reserve through First Security Bank and had placed it, in $100,000 increments, into one-year T-bills. An additional entry showed a portion of Amelia Ball's contribution had purchased $250,000 in treasuries about a week later. The zoo's fiscal condition was what most directors would have killed for.

The only thing unusual on the ledger sheet was a sizable amount set aside for animal purchases in what looked like a separate bank account. Noted beside each entry was a species of animal. The most recent notation, for an African lion, was entered as a totaled amount of $250,000.

Mac sat forward and reread the account entry. With the present cooperation among American and international zoos, purchase of wild animals was not only becoming less and less necessary, but in many cases was illegal. Breeding and loan arrangements made captures from the wild a needless expense. And a purchase of a wild lion was unnecessary and, more importantly, for that amount of money was absurd. Only a breeding pair of black rhino from Africa could justify that degree of cost as zoos scrambled to rescue them from extinction.

But what was even more interesting was that this account was not indicated on the financial statement the Executive Committee had received, this month or last. Mac tapped the end of the pencil against his chin, then reached for the phone. It took a few minutes for Amelia to come on the line.

"Ms. Ball, I'm sorry to disturb you. I've found what looks like the ledger accounting system and compared it against Alex Cristos's financial statement covering the last two months. Even given a few omissions, the bottom line is, Rockland is rock solid.

"As far as I can see, the zoo had been using CDs for investment capital, including your donations, up until H. L. left the fifty-five million. Then it looks like Alex Cristos switched over to treasuries," Mac said.

"That's not unusual. Treasuries have the highest safety rating available, a triple A, and don't have an insured maximum of one hundred thousand dollars, as the CDs do. I would have done the same, considering that amount," she said.

"Well, that's all that I can see has changed. Your donations are logged in on this ledger but not on the last financial sheet. It could have been just a simple oversight."

"My half-million is logged? How was it invested?"

"The ledger shows half went into treasuries, just like H. L.'s money. I can't really pinpoint the rest."

"Mac, now listen carefully. On the ledger, are there any special activity accounts? Especially any set up in the last month or so?"

Mac glanced at the last page again. "Accounts payable all look normal. There is a sizable account set up for animal purchases. Which is a little strange. I wasn't aware we were expanding our population."

Mac heard a sharp laugh on the other end of the phone. "I knew it. My hunch is money from cash donations and money put into treasuries is being journaled into a phony purchasing account. The dummy account is just a way to get the money out of the local bank and accessible. We need to find out who has authority on that account. Whoever's name is on it is behind all this."

"All what?"

"Embezzlement."

Mac stared at the black receiver.

"Treasuries are about as liquid as you can get. The Fed usually holds the notes but will transfer them to any account, anywhere in the Federal Reserve system, that bears the same name as the purchaser's. Those notes can then be sold on the secondary market for cash. We trade more treasuries in this country than we do stocks."

"But wouldn't a bank have to do that?"

"Yes, but a bank would be glad to handle the sale, since they usually take a fat fee for the transaction. The seller would get less money than the note's face value but, in this case, probably wouldn't lose more than ten grand for selling H. L.'s entire fifty-five million. The seller merely signs over a bond power and the buyer goes away thrilled, since he gets the notes at a discount, totally unaware of what is going on. It certainly is worth it for the seller, even with the small loss of value."

Mac whistled softly. "Then Hilton Locke has to be in on this."

"Not necessarily. The treasuries could be wired to any bank, savings and loan, or investment firm, out of state, or even in another country. As long as they have access to the Fed wire system."

"But wouldn't the zoo's auditor notice a bunch of money suddenly disappearing?"

"Since Rockland is privately funded, they are audited only once a year for tax filing purposes. The 990T form. Plenty of time for someone to pocket millions and shuffle off to Buffalo. Or, more likely, South America. We need to know where that phony account is held and whose name is on it."

"I was told Ed Hargreve worked for a bank in New Jersey. Newark, I think. Right before he took the position here."

"Ed Hargreve. . . . Not totally unthinkable. I'll make a few calls." She was gone before he had time to answer.

Mac slowly put the telephone back on the hook. If there was a scheme to embezzle money from the zoo and Stewart had found out, fifty-five million would be well worth a murder. Especially if Hargreve had sixteen committee members to vouch for his whereabouts.

So what if Hargreve didn't look like the murderer type. Most murderers don't exactly cooperate by running around in a goalie mask. Besides, Mac had seen a lot of men kill who weren't the type.

And, let's face it, Mac thought, I'm not exactly swamped with suspects. Okay, so maybe I'm just grabbing at straws. Trying to make anything fit. But if you're about to do free-fall off a cliff—at least when it's unplanned—a straw suddenly looks pretty attractive. Mac felt like a guy teetering at the edge.

So what if Hargreve had killed Stewart? How much time would he have needed to get from the main building to the wolf compound, kill Stewart, and get back to his meeting? And would the other committee members be aware of how much time had elapsed while they were preoccupied with other business? There was only one way to know. Mac collected his flashlight and let himself out of the office.

Arriving at the main building's front door, he checked his watch. He was starting off for the wolf compound at a fast pace when a movement at a window on the second floor caught his eye. Mac ducked back into the shadows of the building.

The silhouette of a figure walked past Hargreve's big office window. Farther back, another shadow moved across the opposite wall. What was Hargreve doing here? He wasn't signed onto the grounds. Mac couldn't remember if the gold Mercedes had been in the parking lot.

As Mac watched, Hargreve walked directly up to the window. Looking out, he appeared to be talking to the person behind him. Mac moved back deeper into the shadows of the flowering shrubbery. Hargreve seemed agitated, turning and waving his arms and pointing a finger at the other person. Slamming his fist on the windowsill, the director stormed away from the window and out of view.

Mac toyed with the idea of sneaking into the building to find out whom the other shadow belonged to, but dismissed it. There was no way to see into Hargreve's office without being seen himself. He'd have to check out the cars in the parking lot on the way out. Security kept a record of all employee cars and Jeff Vincent owed him a favor.

Mac checked his watch again and started out. The walk from the main building to the wolf enclosure took four minutes and ten seconds at a fast clip. Hargreve couldn't have done it any faster and not arrived back at the meeting noticeably winded. Adding a return trip, it would have taken just under ten minutes.

But Hargreve would also have needed time for the actual murder. Stewart's throat had been torn out and the right arm badly mangled. Not exactly a straightforward method of killing, and very time consuming. Only a professional or a lunatic could murder that ruthlessly, then appear unruffled at a business meeting a few minutes later. Mac turned back toward the zoo parking lot.

Deep in thought, Mac almost missed the dark figure who disappeared through the entrance of the pachyderm building's boiler room. Hesitating, Mac glanced over at the administration building. Hargreve's office lights were still on but no one was visible. Mac turned and followed the person into the boiler room.

Stepping cautiously into the hot, noisy room, Mac slowly scanned the area for movement. Squatting down in a small niche inside the doorway, he waited, watching, as he had done so many years ago in an equally hot place. After a few minutes, he stood and crept silently to one of the ten-foot boilers. Peering around, he found the room empty. In the middle of the room, lying on the floor, was a single plastic surgeon's glove.

Ignoring his instincts, he walked over to the glove, looked around, and bent over to pick it up. He sensed too late the brief flash of movement behind him. A split second later pin-points of light exploded as something hard connected with the back of his skull. The cement floor came up to meet him, sur-prisingly soft and welcoming, his legs crumpling beneath him. Mac tried to roll away, to protect his head, but his body wouldn't respond.

A pair of New Balance sneakers walked into his line of vision and up to his right ear. Mac struggled to see the person's face but the white sneakers gradually faded into a speckled gray, then a black nothingness.

•   •   •

From somewhere in the outreaches of his consciousness, Mac was aware of being dragged. An annoyance, it seemed to be happening to someone else, slowly becoming increasingly per-sonal. Groaning against the disturbance of the blissful darkness, Mac tried to shake off the viselike grip that encircled his left arm. As from a long distance he heard a deafening thud that shook the black, enveloping cocoon. He vaguely recognized the sound of the elephant enclosure doors, closing.

The sound helped him focus, as did the scraping of his body along a rough and unyielding surface. He weakly struggled in protest but it had no effect. Opening his eyes to complete dark-ness, he realized he was in the grasp of an elephant trunk. In an instant, Mac was fully alert and fighting for his life.

Mac prayed it wasn't Koko, the big African bull elephant, who had the crushing hold on his arm. He reached out with his free hand to get a feel for the size of the elephant, just as his body was lifted and slammed against the concrete wall. The air rushed out of his lungs in a loud, painful grunt. Gasping, he knew this elephant wasn't Koko. The bull's brute six-ton strength would have shattered every bone in his body on the first bounce.

This elephant was smaller and playing with him like a new toy, tossing him about in pachyderm glee. Mac figured it had to be one of the African females. But being any elephant's object of attention was a life-threatening situation, regardless, and he struggled to free his arm. In response the female swung him effortlessly back and forth in midair. He tried to grab hold of the trunk with his other hand but she shook him loose with her massive head as if he were a bothersome gnat.

Mac felt himself being lifted higher into the air, his arm bones groaning under the crushing pressure. In seconds he could permanently lose the arm. Mac frantically tried to remember the keeper's commands.

"Drop it," he yelled.

His right shoulder took the full impact as he plummeted down onto the hard floor, pain searing inward. Clutching his shoulder, he quickly rolled away from the animal, in the darkness not knowing where he was. Mac knew he was in imminent danger of being crushed, even if by accident. He had to reach the safety zone, a small protected area keepers used in emergencies.

Scrambling forward, he found the wall of the enclosure with his hands and groped his way along, hearing the elephant shuffling closer. An elephant's acute sense of smell is equally efficient in light or dark. She could find him in seconds, he knew. The female was right behind him. Mac had only seconds to find the entrance to the safety zone.

A soft snuffle came up against the back of his neck, sending goose bumps in all directions. The elephant ran her trunk around to his left ear and then under his chin. She would instinctively wrap her trunk around this nearest available part and try to recapture her toy. His neck would snap with the first jerk.

Mac threw himself down onto the floor and crawled, scrabbling, forward. The elephant's foot thudded down inches away from his left leg. The concrete tore at the knees of his pants legs as he lunged ahead, his breath coming in painful rasping gulps. Her snakelike trunk found him again and moved up his inner thigh. Where was the safety zone? Was he going in the right direction?

The elephant's other front foot brushed past Mac's right leg and he knew all four tons of elephant were directly over him now. Her trunk circled around his leg, just above the kneecap. Throwing himself forward in one last desperate dive, Mac crashed into the eight-inch steel posts that guarded the safety zone. Grabbing hold of the posts with both hands, he flung himself between them, slamming face first into the opposite wall of the narrow passageway. The inquisitive trunk followed him into the zone, almost reaching the back of his khaki shirt.

Mac pressed his face into the cool cement wall, his chest heaving, making himself as thin as possible. He groped downward for his walkie-talkie. The belt clip was empty. Turning around, he leaned his sweat-soaked back against the wall and waited for his breathing to return to normal. The female, losing interest, shuffled off into the darkness.

The momentary safety wouldn't last forever. The zone was built to give other keepers time to come to someone's assistance, not to protect a man for the night. Eventually, the elephant would get curious and bored and come back. Her trunk could pull him through the bars in less than the blink of an eye. Sort of like human pasta. Mac tried not to think about it.

How to get out? Even if the door was unlocked, trying to locate the small steel-plated keeper's door in the dark, before the elephant reached him, would be like trying to hit a kiddie pool from the top of the World Trade Center. The other, larger animal door was hydraulically powered with twelve hundred pounds of pressure. Even an elephant couldn't move it. Mac had seen them try.

The winter enclosure was built to withstand the constant assault from the massive creatures. The walls were eighteen feet tall and two feet thick and completely smooth. And without a sledgehammer, breaking through the triple-pane reinforced safety glass of the viewing window would be impossible.

Mac could move down the series of safety zones and then try to figure a way out. The far end of each safety zone opened up into the next elephant's enclosure. All the pens were connected that way so the keepers could travel the entire length of the building without having to go out into the hallway. But in the pitch dark, moving through an elephant's pen was just short of suicide. Especially if one of those elephants was Koko. It would be a very short-lived mistake.

If only he could get to the baby elephant, Bobby. Mac would be safe there—at least from the four-footed animals.

A blast of hot air detonated directly on the front of his khaki shirt. The female was back and ready to play. He couldn't stay there any longer.

He inched himself along the zone to the opposite end. He could hear the scrape of big feet pacing in the connecting pen. He stopped, held his breath, and listened. The animal sounded the size of an armored tank. Mac prayed and stepped into its pen, flattening himself against the wall.

Four tree-sized feet came toward him. The elephant could smell him, but Mac couldn't see the animal. His heart pounded wildly, his breath coming short and fast, as he steeled himself, ready to jump back into the safety zone.

"Like being locked in a damn closet," he muttered. But most closets didn't have huge animals wanting to play with your body. The shuffling sound came closer.

A trunk came out of the darkness and nuzzled up against his cheek. Mac's knees went weak and he felt like shouting. It was a small trunk, Bobby's. Mac ran his hand down the trunk and inside the youngster's mouth, greeting him affectionately, elephant style. The little guy blew gently into the vet's face in response.

Bobby wandered away as Mac sank down onto the step of the safety zone. Whoever had put him in here was both clever and deadly. And not someone who would leave evidence. His attacker would eventually come back and discover he wasn't a grease spot on the enclosure floor. Mac stood up. Moving through the zones wouldn't protect him for long. He had to figure a way out of the building, and fast.

The only possible way out was up. Up the eighteen-foot wall of smooth concrete. The side walls of the enclosure ran straight back to the keeper's hallway, where they joined the back wall, which ran the entire length of the building. At each end of the building was a maintenance ladder that led up to the roof. Once on the roof, he could follow the pachyderm roof to the carnivore compound's roof and to its fire escape.

He had to get on top of the wall. He needed a ladder. Bobby. Although young, the elephant was still a good seven feet tall. Add another few feet of trunk and Mac's own six feet, and he might just make it.

Grasping Bobby by the ear, Mac felt along until he found the wall. Bringing Bobby up to it, he gave the little elephant the command to halt. In the dark, Mac ran his hand down the animal's trunk, hooked his foot, and gave the command to lift. Even at 200 pounds, lifting Mac would be simple for the elephant. It was getting Bobby to let go that had Mac worried.

In the dark, Mac felt himself come off the ground. Balancing his weight, he steadied himself with a hand on the elephant's broad forehead. His other hand followed up the wall, searching for the top edge. He could hear his heart pounding loudly in his ears.

When its trunk was at head level, Bobby stopped, suspending Mac in midair. Mac placed his hand on the wall and stretched upward. Nothing. In the dark he couldn't see if he had missed by an inch or a mile.

Suddenly in the next pen, the sound of the keeper's door creaking open echoed through the compound. Mac fought a feeling of panic. Whoever had put him in here had killed Stewart, and now it was his turn.

Mac whispered to Bobby the command to lift again. Bobby stretched upward, and held. Mac gathered himself and gave one final desperate upward spring, lunging blind in the darkness. He traveled upward and stalled, beginning to fall back, just as his hands caught the top ledge. He fell heavily against the wall, the ragged concrete edge tearing into his hands. Mac heard Bobby move away nervously as he dangled eighteen feet above the enclosure floor.

He swung his leg up and hooked the ledge and clawed himself level and then over. Lying flat on the top of the wall, he listened, his breath disturbing small puffs of dust. The keeper's door in the next pen slammed shut.

Chapter 8

Footsteps walked quickly away from the keeper's door of the next pen and a flashlight beam raked the darkness in searching arcs. Mac flattened himself down in the middle of the wall, making himself as compact as his bulk would allow. If his attacker turned on the house lights, he'd be spotted within minutes. A narrow shaft of light probed inches below where he lay. He forced himself to remain completely still, limiting his breathing to rapid, shallow gulps. Putting his head down, he waited, every fiber tensed.

The footsteps moved systematically down the hallway from pen to pen. After each keeper's door slammed shut, Mac heard the sound of its dead bolt ramming home. A loud curse came from just below him. The footsteps turned and quickened, running down the hallway and out the far door.

Checking the fluorescent hands of his watch, Mac stayed motionless for another fifteen minutes. Bobby and the female stirred restlessly just below him on either side of the wall.

Mac cautiously inched his way along the top of the wall on hands and knees to its junction with the rear wall and turned in the direction of the maintenance ladder. It was slow going but he didn't dare stand for fear of losing his balance on the rough surface. Every so often he'd stop and listen, convinced he had heard his attacker return.

The trapdoor at the top of the ladder gave way to a shove and he crawled out onto the roof. Closing it softly behind him, he paused, soaking in the cool night air, and realized he was shaking. So much for a career in espionage, he thought.

Keeping near the center of the roof, he made his way across to the carnivore building and to the top rung of the fire escape. Pausing again, he waited, listening and watching. His head pounded where a lump had appeared just above the right ear. Each movement caused his shoulder to scream in protest.

He would notify security as soon as he reached a phone, and almost as immediately changed his mind. He knew who was behind this. There was only one man who was connected to Joanne Nordstrom, who was at odds with Donald Stewart, and who wanted Mac's investigations to stop—one man with banking connections. Edward Hargreve.

The director had to be the muscle behind what had been going on. Events like this didn't just happen, they were orchestrated. And that took contacts and money, big money.

The only movement in the evening moonlight was a rat scurrying across the pathway in search of leftovers. Mac climbed quickly down the fire ladder and headed for Hargreve's office at a run. Keeping to the shadows, he ducked and bobbed and remembered a night like this in 'Nam, the moon so bright it looked like midday. He had lost a lot of men that night.

The front door of the main building opened noiselessly. Stepping into the darkened foyer, he heard the macaw start, flapping nervously. Taking the stairs two at a time, he hugged the wall, moving down the hallway toward the partially open office door. Light shone out onto the hall floor in a distorted rectangle. The building was ominously quiet.

Reaching Hargreve's office, he peered around the corner. The room was completely silent and his instincts were back at red alert. He could just barely see the edge of Hargreve's desk. Mac tiptoed over to Claire's desk and picked up a lethal-looking letter opener and moved to the director's door. Reaching forward, he slowly pushed it back against the wall.

Hargreve's desk had been mostly cleared, its lamp hanging precariously over one side. A high-back chair was upside down like a giant, lifeless beetle. In the far corner, the bar had been pulled open, and glasses spilled and broken, revealing an empty safe, its door ajar. Lying beside it on the expensive Oriental rug was Ed Hargreve, a single small-caliber bullet hole punctuating his gray pinstriped suit an inch below the left shoulder blade.

Mac steadied himself against the doorframe, riveted to the spot. Finally shaking himself into action, he stumbled over to Hargreve and felt for a pulse. The man's pupils were dilated and fixed.

Going to the desk, Mac located the phone and dialed security. A second call went to Kirby. Hanging up, he walked numbly back into Claire's office and sat down at her desk. Somehow being there made him feel better.

•   •   •

"Finding dead bodies is getting to be a habit with you," Kirby said from the doorway less than ten minutes later. Uniformed officers formed a half circle behind him.

Mac didn't answer. He thought he had seen all the dead bodies any one person could expect in one lifetime. It hadn't been easy then, either.

"You again?" the medical examiner said as he bustled past, followed by his contingent of assistants.

Mac knew the drill. The office filled up with various police officers efficiently performing their duties. He tried to ignore the suspicious looks. Three deaths in three days and he was present for all of them.

Kirby came out of Hargreve's office jotting things down in his notebook. "Petty cash is gone. Looks like the burglar forced Hargreve to open the safe. Surprised he put up such a fight."

"A robbery? Kirby, you've got to be kidding. There's a *pattern* going on here. You can't see the connection?"

"The only connection I see, I'm lookin' at." The detective continued to scribble as he talked. "Not exactly sure what else is missing. I'll have to talk with the secretary. What's her name?"

"Claire. Claire Burke."

"Ah, right." Kirby glanced at him with a knowing look. "Okay, show me how you found the victim."

Mac followed him into the office.

"I saw the light on in Hargreve's office, so I came in and pushed the door open. This is how I found it. I only touched Hargreve—to see if he was alive—and the phone to call you and security. That's it."

"About what time?"

"Ten thirty-five."

Kirby looked at him closely. "I checked my watch just before I left the pachyderm building. I figure about eight to ten minutes to get here and into the office," Mac said defensively.

"What happened to your head?"

Mac just couldn't bring himself to tell him. Maybe because he had to agree the whole scene looked more than a little incriminating. Again. After all, Hargreve was dead, the office was torn apart, and Mac looked like the loser at a demolition derby. He gingerly touched the goose egg that protruded above his ear. "I connected with a pipe in the boiler room."

"That's it?"

"That's my story."

Kirby's eyes narrowed slightly. "You need to be more careful."

The medical examiner proceeded to chalk out the position

of the body. Mac watched in strange fascination as a stray thought niggled at him, something about Hargreve.

The director's head was turned at an unnatural angle to the side, the right arm thrown overhead, one custom brown wing tip kicked off. Blood had soaked a doughnut around the clean-cut bullet hole.

"His ring. It's gone," Mac said suddenly.

Kirby looked expectantly at the medical examiner, who was finishing up his inspection. The man bent over and picked up Hargreve's limp hand. "He's right. There's an imprint of a ring on the third finger of the victim's right hand."

"Well, that about wraps this up. Obviously Hargreve was forced to open the safe. They struggled and the perpetrator shot him, then emptied the cash drawer and took the ring." The policeman snapped his notebook shut with a satisfied sigh. "I love it when they're neat."

"Then why leave his watch? That Rolex is worth some bucks," Mac said.

"Oh, excuse me, Detective MacIntire," Kirby said. "You have another brilliant theory?"

"Listen, around ten minutes after nine or so I walked by and saw Hargreve standing by that window talking to somebody back here by the desk. It was not a friendly discussion."

"Who was it?" Kirby asked.

"I couldn't see."

"Only one person?"

"I'm not sure. I saw only Hargreve and one other shadow."

"What were they arguing about?"

Mac felt himself getting hot. "I couldn't hear. I could just see Hargreve's arm waving and expressions."

"Oh, so now you read body language."

Mac struggled with his temper. "Okay, have it your way. I'm going home if you're done with me."

Kirby made a show of looking at his watch. "See ya tomorrow."

Mac paused and looked at the detective. "One thing's for sure, Kirby, at least you can't blame *that*"—pointing at the body—"on Toka. Wolves are lousy shots." Mac forced himself to walk out of the office.

•   •   •

The Rover stood where he had left it what seemed like centuries ago. The parking lot was empty except for the assortment of marked and unmarked police cars. And Hargreve's parking spot was vacant.

Mac's shoulder was on fire and it felt as if there was a good chance the right side of his head might fall off. All he wanted was to forget, go home to a nice warm bed, and pretend it didn't matter. More important, pretend he didn't care. He aimed the Rover for home.

Even if Hargreve had been murdered deliberately, it didn't get the wolves off the hook for Stewart's death. Somehow he still had to prove the wolves had been framed, and prove it before tomorrow at closing time.

Who stood to gain by murdering the general manager, Joanne, and now Hargreve? Mac swore to himself. Even Kirby couldn't possibly brush off these killings as unrelated, just a series of unfortunate incidents.

The problem was, other than the videotapes of two different brands of sneakers at two different places at the same time, he had no evidence. No concrete evidence, anyway. And now his number-one prime suspect was bleeding all over the carpeting.

Mac slammed the steering wheel in frustration. Kirby was right about one thing, Mac was in way over his head.

He parked the Rover and let himself into his apartment. Tossing down his keys, he started for the kitchen, hunger finally overpowering fatigue. Opening the refrigerator door, he stared blankly at the empty interior and slowly pushed it shut. He leaned his forehead on the smooth metal, eyes closed.

He had had bad nights before, but when Sara had been alive, he'd known she'd be waiting for him, soft-covered strength, sipping herbal tea. He could almost smell it, hear the clink of the spoon against the cup. They had been partners battling the odds together. The familiar empty ache churned with his hunger.

After Sara had died, he hadn't run from the loneliness, taking up with the first woman who offered sympathy. He had battled on by himself. He needed to be sure the causes they had fought for had been his own causes. So he had proved it to himself, that he could do it solo. But now he didn't want to.

Five minutes later he had located Claire's number in the phone book, dialed it into his call forwarding, and locked the apartment door. He hadn't realized it until just now, but Claire had that same rock-solid feeling as Sara. He felt better already.

●   ●   ●

It was just past midnight when Claire opened the door on the fifth buzz. Eek was doing delirious fur-flying pinwheels over their feet.

"Is this the Salvation Army?"

"You in need of saving, brother?"

"I'd settle for a heating pad and some ice," Mac said, stepping inside and pushing the door closed with his foot. His arms were busy pulling an unresisting Claire to him.

The faint scent of coconut enveloped him in a soft, addictive cloud. Her peach satin housecoat was smooth and cool. She felt good in his arms. She felt safe.

Untangling herself, Claire led him into the living room and pushed him gently down onto the sofa. "That's one terrific-looking lump you got there," she said, disappearing into the next room.

"Thanks."

Claire came out carrying a hot-water bottle tucked under her arm, a bag of ice in one hand, and a stiff Scotch in the other.

"Here. If the first two don't help, I guarantee the third one will." She padded back into the kitchen in her bare feet and returned with a frosted glass of white wine. Switching on some gentle music as she passed, she plopped down on the couch, pulled Eek off Mac's lap, and took a sip.

"Aren't you going to ask?" Mac asked.

"About what?"

"About what happened? My head, this lump?"

"I figure you'll tell me when you're ready."

She said it matter-of-factly and Mac knew she meant it. I couldn't possibly be this lucky in one lifetime, he thought.

"Ed Hargreve's dead."

Claire choked on half-swallowed wine, paling slightly. "When? How? Oh God."

Mac gingerly shifted the ice pack to the other side of the Mount-Everest–sized lump. "Tonight, in his office. He was arguing with someone, I don't know who, and forty-five minutes later I found him dead. Shot. Kirby thinks it was a burglary gone bad."

Claire was silent for a minute. "The grief isn't exactly blowing me away, but still, he didn't deserve to die. I mean, it wasn't like there was anything in that safe. H. L. used to use it for his personal papers and things. I didn't think Ed even knew the combination."

"His diamond ring's gone too. But, you know, I don't think it was a burglary. Hargreve was really having it out with somebody and you usually don't argue with a robber, especially if he's brought a gun to the party."

Claire nodded. Mac had the Scotch almost to his lips when an icy tingle at the nape of his neck stopped his hand. "How'd you know the safe was open?" he asked.

Claire shifted uncomfortably on the sofa. "Well, ah, I just assumed . . . what else would a burglar be after?"

Mac looked at her suspiciously, an unsettling mix of conflicting emotions battling.

"Mac, why are you looking at me like that?"

He forced himself to smile. He forced himself to ignore the thought that had turned him cold.

"Do the police have any idea who did it?" Claire asked, breaking the lengthening silence.

Mac shrugged and shook his head, focusing back on the puzzle. He had to be overlooking some important piece of the big picture. Something that would make all of this fall neatly into place. He hated puzzles. "By the way, I hope you don't mind but I forwarded my phone calls here. I'm expecting an important call from a guy in New Jersey, who'll shed some light on what's going on. I hope."

"Gee," she said, a small smile tugging at the corners of her mouth. "I was thinking about doing exactly the opposite." She reached over and switched off the table lamp and pulled his face down to hers.

Any idea of going back to his own apartment that night evaporated into a distant, fragrant memory.

●   ●   ●

He followed her down the hall and waited for the inevitable wave of guilt. The guilt that always muscled its way in, interposing itself between him and whatever particular woman he was with. Images of loving Sara would dance in the darkened theater of his mind, accompanied by the impatient rustle of bed linens. He had learned to partially ignore it, well enough to go through the motions, but it always left him dissatisfied. Not with the woman, but with himself.

Claire's housecoat whispered down into a pile on the plush bedroom rug. She smiled and beckoned. He stepped close and waited, anticipation tempered, steeling himself for the ache. But it didn't come.

He ran his hand down the fine silken skin of the small of Claire's back and felt them both respond. She nuzzled close into the circle of his arms as he eased her down onto the bed.

For the first time, Sara didn't shimmer at the edges of his passion. Instead, Claire was solidly there, real and smooth, soft and ample. He savored the exploration of her curves and rises and found a lost intoxication. The cool of the sheets gave way to mutual hypnotic fire.

●　　●　　●

It always started the same way, the dream. Sara beside him, walking on the foam-flecked sand, the warm sun on his skin. They laugh. But this time, reaching for her, she pulls away. With her small hand she lovingly strokes his cheek. Turning, she walks up the beach. He tries to follow but she waves him back, motioning him to stay. She smiles. Her tiny form recedes into the distant mist of ocean spray.

Heart-wrenching sadness washes over him, yet he knows it's time. Mac stands on the beach, waves mining the sand from beneath his feet, letting her go.

●　　●　　●

A persistent ringing woke Mac just after two-thirty. Claire stirred sleepily beside him, groping for the phone.

"Do you usually have late calls?" he asked. She shook her tousled head and he picked up the receiver.

"Hello?"

"MacIntire? Rorke here. I got it and you won't believe it." The PI's voice was loud and eager and Mac could feel the crooked man's excitement.

"I need whatever you got, and fast," Mac said.

"I can't say for sure how Stewart was killed, but I'm pretty damn sure why. Stewart had something on Hargreve and Cristos, all right. Big time. Your director is a very naughty boy. Past and present.

"He and Cristos were under suspicion for conspiracy to embezzle—that article you found. Cristos by that teamsters' union down here and Hargreve by the local bank. The officials couldn't nail down any concrete proof, but both men stepped down from their positions. Some of the rank-and-file are claiming H. L. paid off the various brass to get his son, and the Hargreve name, off the hook.

"As for Cristos, he has a long history of shady business dealings, some even mob related, and a healthy reputation for resorting to violence. He teamed up with Hargreve while working for the union. Cristos was their chief financial officer.

"But that's just the warm-up. There's been some real heavy stuff going on at the zoo. I've got enough dirt on Hargreve to bury him," Rorke said.

"That should come in handy. Hargreve's dead," Mac said.

There was a long silence on the other end.

"Rorke? Did you hear me? Hargreve was shot tonight in his office. Kirby thinks he tangled with a burglar."

"Where's Cristos?"

"I don't know."

"Tell Kirby he needs to locate Cristos, and quick. There's a wild card still missing to all this that I'm tracking down. The whole scam's bigger than just embezzling a few bucks. I'm meeting with a guy in an hour who says he can tie it all up for me. If it's what I think it is, we're going to blow this case right out of the water."

"Then Stewart was murdered—and not by wolves?"

"This guy tonight will tell me who, but probably not how. It could still have been the wolves. You know, the jailer opens the door and throws the Christian to the lions. So who killed him, the man or the animal?"

"Oh, great." Mac felt the sickening thud of discouragement.

"I'm flying back as soon as I finish with this guy. Where will you be?"

"Name it."

"If I take the shuttle, I'll be at your apartment in two and a half hours. Be there." Rorke hung up.

Mac rolled over and nestled Claire back onto his shoulder and put his face down into her dark-brown hair.

"Well, that's it. Rorke couldn't get enough evidence to clear the wolves. He knows someone killed Stewart, or at least arranged it, but couldn't rule out the wolves completely."

"Mac, you did everything humanly possible. You sacrificed your job for those wolves. No one could accuse you of not giving it your best." Claire planted a kiss on his cheek and climbed out from under the sheets and headed for the bathroom. "Now that I'm awake, mind if I take a shower?"

As the water ran, Mac went over every bit of information he had. But all he came up with was an assortment of unrelated tidbits. H. L. and Joanne's secret romance, a misidentified snake donated by a Ralph Danesto, different sneakers, abnormal wolf behavior, a mysterious zoo bank account, embezzlement at a New Jersey union, and Joanne's ominous warning on the floor of the front office. Why should Joanne try to tell him about H. L.'s ring when she was fighting for her life? Nothing about any of this made sense.

And someone clearly wanted him out of the picture. But who? He took the pillow and put it over his head, hoping to stop the endless circuit of futile thinking.

Claire's voice came from the bathroom as she stepped from the shower. "You committing suicide in there?"

Mac uncovered his head and watched her reflection in the bathroom mirror. She slowly smoothed talcum powder in long strokes down her body. Her silhouette was backlighted, strong, tall, and healthy, the large puff following each accented line. The scent of coconut wafted out to him.

"I like that smell, is it the powder?"

"Yeah, messy but worth it," she replied.

Powder. It felt like a shot dead between the eyes.

He grabbed for the phone and glanced at the clock. While he dialed Kirby's precinct number, he prayed the cop was still there, still working, still annoying his wife. The detective answered on the eighth ring.

"This better be better than just good, MacIntire."

"We need to check something out fast. When I found Stewart in the wolf enclosure, he had on surgeon's gloves. Right? Well, when the medical examiner took them off Stewart, I saw the powder on the outside. He wiped his hands on his pants."

"You call me at three in the morning to talk about powder?"

"If Stewart had put the gloves on himself, the powder would have been on the inside, not the outside. It's to keep the gloves from sticking when the hands perspire. The only way the examiner could have gotten powder on his hands like that was if the gloves had been put on inside out."

"So?"

"Would you put the powder side facing out if you were washing windows? Stewart didn't put those gloves on himself. They were put on him, probably after he was dead.

"I already have proof there was someone in New Balance sneakers at the wolf compound at the time of death and I'm willing to bet, if your lab checks, they'll find another set of fingerprints somewhere in the powder coating.

"The killer pulled the gloves off after the murder and, when he did, the gloves turned inside out. Then he slipped them on Stewart to make it look convincing—that he was washing windows. And it was someone who *knows* the zoo. Someone who knows we always wear gloves when using chemicals. It's policy."

There was a long pause before Kirby spoke. "That is the most half-assed idea I've heard in a long time. Give it up, Doc, the wolves did it. Now let it go."

Mac decided to gamble. "Some people could have walked away from Fang, lying there on the side of the road. Just let a cat die and not given it a second thought. But you didn't. You brought him to me, went out of your way, to give him a fighting chance. That's all I'm asking for, Kirby, give the wolves a fighting chance. Just one last shot."

"Jesus, here comes the violin music."

"Check the gloves. Think about it. Then cancel the disposal."

"Why should I?" Kirby demanded.

"Because if individuals don't care, don't fight to protect what can't protect itself, then we're all screwed. We are all helpless, eventually, sometime, at some point. Somebody's got to care."

The detective didn't answer.

"Besides, Rorke called from New Jersey. He said that Hargreve was involved in something big. Rorke'll be back in a few hours. He said to tell you to locate Alex Cristos and fast."

"Cristos? The financial officer?"

"That's the message."

"Now Rorke I believe." Kirby covered the receiver and relayed the information to someone behind him.

"There's one more favor I need," Mac said.

"Oh, Christ."

"I need to know exactly what was returned with H. L.'s body when they flew it home from Africa. A list of his personal effects."

"What the *hell* does that have to do with anything?" Kirby shouted.

"Humor me." Mac hung up on Kirby, who was still swearing.

Chapter 9

It was just after five in the morning when Mac pulled into his apartment's parking space. The sun was a faint blush of pink at the bottom of a semidarkened sky. In a few minutes it would burst up over the horizon, launching millions of people, like overdressed hamsters, onto their daily wheel. The Rover coughed to a standstill and Mac climbed out, a little sleep deprived.

He fumbled with his key ring as he walked, head down, toward the front door. The early-morning light threw a dark shadow across the entryway, obscuring a full view. It wasn't until Mac was at the door, reaching for the knob, that he realized the door was open.

He took a step backward. Locking doors was totally automatic, drilled into him by years of working with dangerous animals. And especially since his office break-in, he had been very certain to lock that door the night before. He stepped to the side of the doorway and listened. Dead silence. In the back of his head familiar alarm bells shrieked at full volume.

Mac took a cautious step into the apartment, half crouching.

The living room was dim and it took a couple of seconds for his eyes to adjust.

Rorke sat on the sofa, head propped back, mouth open, hands folded at the belt line. Sitting unexpectedly straight. Too straight for a man with a bad back.

"Rorke?" The man didn't move. "Rorke?" Mac hissed, louder.

Mac looked quickly around the room and edged over to the hallway. Stepping across into the empty kitchen, he peered down toward the bedroom, slipped off his shoes, reached into the open closet, took hold of his favorite baseball bat, and tiptoed noiselessly down to the bedroom. Scanning the bathroom and then the closet, he moved through each room until he was convinced no one else was there. Returning to the living room, he locked the front door.

A tentative finger on the side of Rorke's neck confirmed his fear. Neatly folded into the dead man's hand was a note that read, "Get ready. You're next."

Mac knew Kirby's phone number by heart.

•　　•　　•

"I ought to take you in for questioning. Suspicion of homicide," the detective said as he stood over Mac, who was sitting at his kitchen table. Mac put his head down into his hands. He couldn't blame Kirby, it looked bad.

"I told you, Kirby, Rorke called from New Jersey. He told me to meet him. I got here a little after five and the front door was open. Found him just like that, with the note stuck in his hand. Then I called you. . . . And, yes, that *is* my story."

"It's time you told me everything, MacIntire," Kirby said, pulling out a chair and sitting down. The morgue crew was going about their duties in the next room. Mac was getting to know them on a first-name basis and he didn't much like it.

"What I got is a bunch of nothing. Rorke said he was going to meet a guy in Newark who'd tie it all together. But he never said who or what, just that Hargreve and Cristos were into something at the zoo. Bigger than we thought. Maybe Rorke took notes."

"His notebook is missing. Okay, start from the top."

Mac tipped back in the flimsy metal chair. "Let's use my theory. All the deaths must be connected, and planned. It's just too much of a coincidence. Joanne Nordstrom gets bitten by a misidentified snake in a box with a bottom that's been purposely weakened. I go to give her the antivenin and the refrigerator's suddenly dead, so the stuff's no good. She tries to tell me something about H. L.'s ring, but dies before she can. Joanne turns out to be H. L.'s longtime lover and surprise heir to a ton of money. Edward takes the job he's always hated. He hires Alex Cristos, a guy he worked with in New Jersey under suspicious circumstances.

"Stewart told me he thought Hargreve was up to something—then I find Stewart dead in the wolf pen. I start nosing around and poisonous spiders throw a reunion in my office. A pair of Nike sneakers—the security guard's—show up on videotape at the ape house but a pair of New Balance sneakers are at the wolf enclosure, at the same time as Stewart's death. I get knocked out by that same pair of New Balance sneakers, get thrown into an elephant pen, and escape in time to find Hargreve part of the rug pattern."

"Wait a minute, what about you in the elephant pen?" Kirby asked.

"Gets real exciting in the dark. That's how I got that lump on my head."

Kirby's face took on an unusual flush. "What else haven't you told me?"

"Nothing, honest. You already know Rorke went to Jersey

to check out the newspaper article I found in Stewart's office. He learned that Edward and Cristos had been under suspicion for embezzlement. Nobody could really prove anything, apparently. There's some question whether H. L. got them out of it. I found what could be a dummy bank account at Rockland, but I can't definitely prove that."

"Who else knew about Rorke going to Newark?"

Mac thought a minute. "Hargreve. I told him yesterday when I went to see him, or was that this morning? I'm losing track." Mac rubbed his weary eyes. "Anyway, he wanted me to report back to him about what I found."

"Did you?"

"No, *he* was my prime suspect. He had had a huge fight with Stewart. Joanne was his father's lover and inherited some of what Ed might have considered his money. He was the only person who was directly connected to both victims. . . . Pretty weak, huh?"

"You could say that."

"Anyway, Hargreve threatened to fire me if I continued poking around."

"He fired you?"

"More like future tense. Well, actually, I'm not sure, seeing as Hargreve's dead. My termination was supposed to be effective as of twelve hours from now."

"I'd say that puts you back on the suspect list, my friend." Kirby flipped his notebook shut with a click.

"Kirby, that's hardly enough motive to kill Hargreve. And it wouldn't account for Rorke. Or Stewart. Or Joanne. Or explain who was in the other sneakers. I'd hardly film myself."

"Maybe." The detective stood up and stuffed the notebook into his pocket. "We still haven't found Cristos or that snake donor, Ralph Danesto. But the FBI's working on Danesto. Their ID should be back in a few hours. We're also checking out your videotapes. Do I need to give you a bit of advice,

MacIntire? I'd stick around." Kirby looked at his watch. "See you at closing."

It was going to be one hell of a long day.

• • •

Shortly after the last of the police stomped out of Mac's apartment, the phone's ringing erased any remaining hope for sleep.

"Dr. MacIntire? This is Esther, the docent director. Sorry to disturb you, but something's up with Molly. I'm pretty sure she's in labor."

"What's she doing?"

"She's been pacing around her cage for the past hour or so. She's moved her nest a few times. And has just started some arm shaking."

"Any contractions?"

"Not that I can see on the monitor. But William Decker's with her now."

"Decker? He's there?" Mac checked his watch. It read just past six-thirty.

"Yes, he told me to call you."

"I'll be right there," Mac said, hung up, and practically ran through the shower.

Fifteen minutes later he was standing in the monitoring room watching Molly pacing restlessly about her private cage. Because her last infant had died of an infection, Molly was in a separate area, away from the other gorilla families.

Every few minutes she would stop, sit perfectly still for a few seconds, vigorously shake her arms, then resume pacing. Mac could see the back of Decker's head as he sat beside the gorilla's cage, occasionally offering her water.

"How long has Decker been here?" Mac asked.

"About four hours now. Came in around three this morning. Said he just had a feeling about her," Esther replied.

Molly reached down into her nest and grabbed a handful of

hay and patted it to her chest. Mac could see Decker's mouth moving, his gestures slow and careful, as he talked to the ape through the bars.

Mac reached for the walkie-talkie and softly called Decker. On the monitor he saw Decker unclip the radio from his belt.

"How's she doing?" Mac asked.

"Okay. She was in early labor when I got here. Been doing a lot of touching and tasting and in the past hour has had some strong contractions. But I can't see any dilation yet."

"You think she'll let me come in the room? I don't want to get her upset."

"She'll do fine. So far she's real relaxed."

Mac left Esther to continue with her recordings, entered the ape room quietly, and squatted down beside Decker. Molly eyed the two men cautiously and then resumed her nest building. Mac let out his breath and sat down on the cold concrete next to the pen.

"I figure she's been in labor about four and a half hours now. Can't figure why she's not further along," Decker said, watching the gorilla closely.

"Could be a big infant. Or maybe it's in a strange position. Molly's records say she delivered easily three years ago. The problem was the infant's bacterial infection. Not a birthing problem," Mac replied.

Decker nodded, not taking his eyes off the ape. He spoke to her quietly, a deep resonance added to his voice. Mac glanced at Decker. There was an unusual softness to the burly keeper, an unexpected gentleness.

"There's still some time before I start getting worried," Mac said. He leaned his shoulder against the bars and settled in for the wait.

By eleven, Mac had begun to pace. Molly was in heavy labor, her discomfort clearly evident in her eyes. Her arm shaking had increased but there was no sign of the birth progressing. And in the past hour Molly had begun to refuse liquids.

Decker sat motionless on the hard floor, watching quietly. From time to time he would call softly to encourage Molly. Mac impatiently ran his hand through his hair.

An uncomplicated gorilla birth usually took no more than three hours. Molly's was now almost three times that. Something was wrong.

"I'm going to call the obstetrician. He can start setting up for a caesarean section. We may have to take this infant," Mac said and started for the phone.

"Hang on, Doc. Give her just a little more time."

"I can't take the chance, Decker. I may lose my wolves today, but I'm sure as hell not going to lose Molly."

Decker looked down at the floor and then back at Mac. "I know, but I think she can do it. She's trying so hard. We've got to give her a chance." He scuffed the heel of his boot across the cement. "Nature's a good system. It's humans who keep mucking it up."

Mac stared at Decker as if he were seeing himself. "You think man will ever figure that out?"

Decker gave him a cynical sneer. "Not a chance."

"So, then what are you doing here?"

Decker shrugged and stared at Molly. "Guess the beast in me can relate to her somehow. I figure animals are about the only thing you can really trust. Everyone else will eventually lie to you."

Mac studied the keeper for a long count. "Okay, she has one more hour, that's it. Then I'm calling in the OB."

It was the longest sixty minutes Mac could remember. Even pacing didn't help. Decker sat, solidly confident, beside the cage, whispering to Molly with every contraction. It made Mac feel rattled, like an overly expectant father.

Mac checked his watch again. Molly's labor had now been going on at least nine hours. He pulled open his treatment bag and took out the tranquilizer gun and Dr. Greenspan's phone number.

"Sorry, Decker. She's had long enough. I can't risk losing her and the infant. I'm going to knock her down so she'll be ready when the OB arrives."

Decker stood slowly and clenched the cage gate with both fists. Leaning forward, he put his face between the bars. "Come on, Molly, you can do it, girl. Damn it, Molly, push!"

The gorilla looked up from the hay she was cradling in her arms and pursed her lips. She rose and walked to the far side of the pen. Squatting down in the corner, she turned and looked at Decker with large, bloodshot eyes. With the next contraction, Molly bore down. Nothing.

"Good girl, Molly, do it again," Decker crooned.

A gush of fluid came with the next contraction, preceding the brief appearance of a dark round shape at Molly's groin.

"That's it, girl, do it. *Push!*" Decker was gripping the bars, standing forward on his toes.

Mac grabbed his field glasses, sidled over to the cage, quickly lay down on the floor, and watched. With the next contraction he saw the infant's head crown, surrounded by the slick, gray amniotic sack. Decker was practically shouting.

A third short push delivered a huge flood of amniotic fluid and the slippery, breathing infant into the female's waiting hands.

Within seconds Molly was cleaning the infant's nose and mouth as the infant wiggled and flailed. Mac quickly checked the color of the baby's mouth through the glasses. A healthy, rosy pink. Soft mewling sounds came from the dark bundle the female held gently in her hands. Bending over, Molly severed the umbilical cord with her teeth and sat down to carefully inspect her baby. The baby cuddled immediately into its mother's chest.

Mac sat up and hastily wiped unexpectedly moist eyes. He looked at Decker. The burly keeper was grinning from one ear to the other. He extended his huge paw-sized hand down to Mac and swung him to his feet.

"I knew she could do it. Way to go, Molly. Damn, that was great." He pumped Mac's hand enthusiastically. "Mother Nature can do it, given a chance. That infant looks big, too. I'd guess around four and a half, maybe five pounds. Probably why it took her so long."

The two men watched the mother and baby with the satisfied air of paternal pride.

"You were right," Mac said. "And they look in good shape. But I think I'm going to hang around to make sure they stay that way." Mac checked his watch. "Listen, Decker, why don't you go home and get some sleep. . . . And thanks for the help."

Decker nodded, picked up his flashlight, and stopped at the door. "Listen, Doc, good luck with the wolves this afternoon. I mean that. If anybody can figure out a way to clear them, it's you." Decker turned and disappeared through the door.

Mac wasn't sure anything could clear the wolves now, much less him. Only a sliver of time remained until closing and his deadline with Kirby.

Chapter 10

Mac wasn't squeamish. Two tours of 'Nam had taken care of that. His job as a medic had been to care for the wounded, but when he had to, he had left the enemy looking like a bad road kill, without even a backward glance.

It had never been the men who fought back that bothered him. It had been the defenseless. The incidental casualties of the larger scheme. Just like the wolves now, pawns in someone's deliberate chess game.

He stood at the wolf compound and looked at Toka and felt the old fire-eating anger. Mac began to pace back and forth in front of the enclosure. There had been no word from Kirby. In Mac's treatment bag were lethal doses of the tranquilizer M99, one for each wolf, in case the lab had found nothing. The lives of the wolves depended on those lab results, their last chance.

Sweat ran down his back despite the cool afternoon air. He shed his khaki jacket and tried to walk off the knot in his stomach. It seemed inconceivable that he was going to have to put down the very animals he had come here to save. A small wood chip flew off the gate's upright as his heavy work boot angrily connected. He wanted to rip it out of the ground.

Toka sat in the shadow of a small scrub bush watching him

intently, the pack waiting for their leader's signals. Mac opened the gate and stepped into the enclosure, closed the gate behind him, and cautiously walked to the middle of the open area. He sank down onto the ground, avoiding any eye contact with the old wolf. Nonchalantly Mac picked up a small twig and began to idly draw circles in the dry dirt. One of the younger wolves stood up, eager to come closer, curiosity overtaking caution.

Toka rose and moved forward, ears up, tail high. Mac kept his head down in appropriate deference. The big male angled to one side, coming within arm's reach, and sniffed the man from knee to boot. Mac forced himself to remain confident but nonaggressive. Satisfied, Toka lowered his tail, yawned, stretched his full length, and lay down. The pack relaxed.

Mac let his breath out slowly. He was now even more certain these wolves, hand-reared by Stewart, would never have attacked unless cornered or fighting for their lives.

"You got some kind of death wish?" Kirby's voice came from behind him.

Mac looked over his shoulder, stood slowly, and left the enclosure. Kirby was leaning casually on the wooden fencing.

"Course a guy who did what you did can't be wrapped too tight anyway. A Silver Star, huh? Who woulda figured," Kirby continued, scrutinizing Mac.

Mac shrugged. "Our side didn't seem to mind. You've been busy doing your homework."

"Just thought I'd check you out."

"So, where are we?" Mac asked impatiently.

"You tell me."

"If the wolves were going to attack anybody, it would have been me, just then, not Stewart. But I can't prove that. So, now what?"

Kirby stood, one arm draped over the fence, with a smirk painted across his face. Mac resisted the urge to personally erase

it, yanked open his treatment bag, pulled out the loaded tranquilizer gun, and strode to the gate. "Let's get this over with,"
he growled.

"It's up to you."

"Why is that suddenly?"

"Lab found fingerprints on the gloves."

"In the powder?"

Kirby nodded. "A partial imprint at the edge of the wrist.
Right where you'd hold it as you pulled it on."

"You mean I don't have to . . . the wolves are cleared?"

"Let's just call it a temporary stay of execution. The lab sent
the fingerprints for ID. Meanwhile I'm going to check them
against any keepers here who could have had access. The iden-
tification should be back by morning. Those suckers"—gesturing toward the pack—"aren't out of the woods yet."

"Any luck on finding that Danesto guy?"

Kirby shook his head, yawning. "Still looking for Cristos,
too. Probably with some babe." Kirby yawned again.

"Don't you ever go to bed?"

"Only when I'm so tired I don't know who's in it with me."
He turned to go. "Oh, I got that list of H. L. Hargreve's per-
sonal effects. Not much came back. A few toiletries, a watch,
Nikon camera, binoculars. That sort of stuff." He pulled a
computer print-out from his pocket and shoved it at Mac.
"Here, knock yourself out, I'm going home."

Mac quickly scanned the list as Kirby disappeared down the
asphalt pathway. There were about ten items, mostly personal.
And one glaring omission—the one he had been looking for—
the gold, two-carat, South African diamond ring had not been
returned with the body. And if it hadn't come home with
H. L., how did his loving son, Edward, get it?

•   •   •

Toka turned, ears up, signaling someone's arrival, as Claire appeared at the bend in the path. Mac reread the list that Kirby had given him and stuffed it into his treatment bag.

"You're smiling. That's good," she said.

Mac pulled her into his arms and gave her a resounding kiss.

"Mac, somebody could see us!"

"There's a good chance I don't work here anymore, remember?"

She gave him a playful thump in the stomach, pulled away reluctantly, and sat down on the viewing bench. "So what happened? I just saw Kirby leaving."

"The police found fingerprints on Stewart's surgeon's glove. They haven't traced them to anyone specific, but it gave their killer-wolf theory what's called 'reasonable doubt.' "

"So, looks like your crusade is about over."

"Not really. Even if the wolves are exonerated, it doesn't prove who killed Stewart. I owe it to him to find out. Which brings us back to the same problem. A bunch of unrelated stuff that I can't tie together. I don't know, maybe I should check out Hargreve's office."

"The police looked through the office pretty thoroughly, and Kirby went over it again this morning by himself. He says Ed just ran up against the wrong burglar."

"Kirby says a lot of things," Mac said.

"Uh-huh."

"What is that supposed to mean?"

"You two are very much alike."

"I don't consider that a major compliment."

"You two blow so much smoke you're practically on fire."

"What! I say exactly what I mean."

Claire just smiled.

"I'm glad that's amusing. Meanwhile I need to figure out how Hargreve was in here last night. Other than the docent watch,

I was the only person signed in at the security booth—and Hargreve definitely wasn't arguing with himself. How could he be here and not logged in?"

"Easy, his entrance."

"His what?"

"Oh, you know Ed, he considered himself above the riffraff. Thought logging in and out was beneath a director, so he had a special entrance cut in right behind the main building. He came and went as he pleased. I'll show you." They headed for the main building.

The sidewalk branched off just as it reached the corner of the building nearest the North American habitat. One well-used side continued to the front door; the other, newer part continued around the back, partially hidden by a mass of flowering rhododendron.

Claire led the way. Fifteen feet from the rear of the building was the perimeter's chain-link fencing. Neatly cut and welded into it was a gate, secured with a combination padlock. Directly opposite the new gate was the rear door of the main building.

"Where does that door lead?" Mac asked.

"To a staircase that goes up to the second floor and opens onto the hall, directly across from my office. This door takes the same key as the front. Hargreve usually parked just on the other side of the fence. He could just unlock the gate and come into the building and to his office by this door."

"Who else knew about this gate?"

"I'm not sure who all knew. But I think Hargreve and Cristos were the only ones who used it."

"So they could come and go from the grounds without anyone seeing them. And so could anyone else who had the combination. Does security check it on their rounds?"

"They must. Right?" Claire looked at him quizzically.

"You're one hell of a partner, there, partner," Mac said, planting a playful swat on her backside. "I need to check out something. See you tonight?"

She grinned up at him and gave him a telling kiss.

He waited as she unlocked the rear door with her key and disappeared up the stairway.

•   •   •

The lack of sleep was beginning to catch up with Mac as he stopped off at the cafeteria. The room was half full of staff. A few waved; most put their heads down and pretended they didn't see him. Choosing a doughnut and a cup of coffee, Mac joined Decker, who was sitting alone in a booth by the windows.

"How's it going?" Decker asked.

"I've had better."

"Heard you got fired."

"Good news travels fast."

"Especially around here. You found Hargreve?"

Mac nodded, taking a bite of doughnut. "Guess this means he won't change his mind about my employment. You seen Cristos?"

"Not since last night."

Mac paused. "You saw Cristos last night?"

"Yeah, around nine-thirty or so. He was stopped at a light in town, right at the entrance ramp to Route 3. In-bound. I was sitting at the light across the street."

Mac tried to look casual. "Probably taking some honey into Boston. Hear he's a high roller."

Decker shook his head. "He was alone and in a big hurry in Hargreve's Mercedes. That's what made me notice him. Kinda hard to miss that ride."

Mac finished his coffee in a gulp and hurriedly excused himself. Two of the keepers added their farewells on Mac's way out the door. They seemed to be getting used to losing people.

•   •   •

The sun was beginning to travel the last remaining feet into the distant hilltops of eastern Massachusetts. Another hour and it would be dark and Mac could ask some private questions of Jeff Vincent. After that, he'd call it quits. Technically he no longer worked at the zoo. By morning Hilton Locke would be in command again, until another director could be found, and the guards would have their orders to treat Mac like any other visitor.

Mac ambled back to his office. He sat down in his ancient office chair and looked around. It had been a great dream, and even better opportunity, and in less than a month it had flamed itself to dust. He propped his feet up just as the phone rang.

"MacIntire?"

"Detective Kirby, how nice of you to phone."

"Didn't think you'd still be on the clock."

"Finishing up a few things. I'll be picking up Fang shortly and heading home to join the unemployed. Just another economic statistic."

"Thought you'd want to know the medical examiner said Rorke had been dead over an hour, maybe two, before you say you found him. Killed with a garrote. Real professional. Murdered somewhere else and brought to your apartment."

"How thoughtful," Mac said.

"Yeah, well, that news doesn't exactly take you off the suspect list, considering your military background. But I assume there's someone who can attest to your whereabouts between three and four this morning."

"In the flesh."

"I bet. And tonight? The same person? Just in case I have to arrest you?"

"Knock first."

Kirby hung up laughing.

•　　　•　　　•

Night had fallen and Mac gathered up a few pieces of his medical equipment, added them to the treatment bag, and headed for the security booth. Jeff Vincent would have just finished his first set of rounds and Mac wanted to get this over with.

The security office was empty as Mac signed out. He glanced quickly through the other time cards. He was the only person still logged in. Turning to go, Mac heard voices, laughing, coming from the rear of the building.

He followed the sound down the narrow hallway to the door of the men's locker room. Jeff Vincent was sitting on a bench in front of a row of beige lockers, lacing up a pair of new brown work boots.

"You finally got 'em," Mac said, stepping into the room.

Jeff looked up, startled. "Hey, Doc, yeah, finally. Course now that Hargreve's toasted I probably don't need them. Figures, huh?"

"Just think how impressed the new director will be," Mac replied.

"Whoever that is," a voice said from around the end of the metal lockers. Toweling off his sweaty face, Nat Watermann stepped around the corner wearing the bottom half of a jogging suit.

Mac looked from Watermann to Vincent and noticed the young guard beginning to turn an unnatural crimson.

"Thought you'd gone home, Nat," Mac said.

"Ah, well, Jeff and I jog his rounds right after closing time." Watermann smiled and leaned casually against a locker door as Jeff took longer than necessary to finish tying his boot.

The silence lengthened until Mac turned to go. "Sounds healthy to me. Well, take it easy, fellas, this is my last day."

Jeff stood a little too quickly and extended his hand. As Mac reached to accept it, something white caught his eye. Glancing down he saw the letters "NB" stitched on the side of Watermann's sneakers.

In a flash Mac had Watermann up against the locker, hands at his throat, the keeper's feet off the floor. Watermann had been present when both Joanne and Stewart died, in the hallway when the spiders showed up in Mac's office, and Watermann's car had still been in the parking lot the night Hargreve was shot. Watermann had been there for it all, the artist viewing his handiwork. Rage tore at Mac, screaming for retribution.

"You bastard," Mac growled through clenched teeth. "I'm going to jam your teeth down your throat, then I'm going to call Kirby and you're gonna rot in jail. You killed Stewart."

Mac heard Jeff Vincent's sharp intake of air behind him. "Wait a minute, Doc, you got it wrong. Honest. Nat didn't kill Stewart."

Watermann seemed frozen in place on the locker. "MacIntire, I swear to God, I didn't kill him," Watermann said.

"Whoever did wore New Balance sneakers. That same person tried to use me for elephant bedding. And you, pal, are sporting the same fashion statement."

"Put him down," Jeff Vincent said quietly. "He didn't do it. He was with me when Stewart was killed."

Mac looked at the guard over his shoulder. Watermann hung motionless in his hands like a limp puppy.

"We always run together right after supper. You told me you saw my sneakers, the Nikes, on the ape film? I couldn't have been at the wolf compound for another hour or more. You can even check the time clocks I had to hit on my rounds. I was right on schedule that night, and, well, Nat was with me the whole time."

Mac let Watermann slide down to the floor. The keeper didn't move, his eyes big and wary.

"Besides, I just bought those sneakers for Nat yesterday when I got these boots. Here, I've still got the receipt. And the store clerk should remember us." The young guard took a rumpled piece of paper out of his wallet with trembling fingers and held it out.

Mac looked from one man to the other, and then took the store receipt. Both pairs of shoes were clearly printed, the sale dated yesterday, two days after Stewart was killed.

He handed the slip back to the guard. "Sorry. Guess this whole thing has me overreacting. But how come, Watermann, you're not logged in or out?"

"We, ah, don't want to make it public. That I'm here with Jeff, if you know what I mean." Watermann glanced away and then down at his foot.

Mac cleared his throat and turned for the door. "Right. Oh, one more thing, Jeff. Ed Hargreve's private entrance. Is it checked on your rounds?"

"If you mean going by a padlocked gate, checking. Anybody who knows the combination could come and go a million times and unless I happened to hit on him at the very time he was coming through it—" Jeff shrugged.

"And the night Hargreve was killed, no one except the docent watch and me was logged in?"

"Nope. No one was on the grounds except you, the docent, and Nat, and he was with me." Jeff glanced nervously over at Watermann, who had sat down heavily on the wooden bench. "You aren't gonna say anything to O'Malley, are you? I mean, I'm still doing my job."

"I don't work here anymore, remember?" Mac replied. "By the way, that favor you owe me? I've got my cat in the nursery but I can't take him home just yet. If I come back later, will you bring him to the gate for me?"

The young guard hastily agreed. Mac left the security building, tossed his treatment bag into the back of the Rover, and drove off. Another screaming, face-smacking dead end, he thought.

•   •   •

It was depressing all the way around. He couldn't seem to pick the right path through the maze. Mac mulled over the possibilities for the hundredth time.

If someone human had killed Stewart, how did they do it? The manager's wounds were not made by the usual weapons. Gun, knife, or club. Mac had seen and treated those kinds of wounds in 'Nam. He'd even seen the aftermath of explosives. Nothing simple like that would have made Stewart's throat injury or, more importantly, left teeth marks. Stewart's arm had had a perfectly shaped horseshoe set of imprints that would have made a dentist euphoric.

Mac ran his hand through his hair. Around and around he went, like a tiger chasing its tail. He turned the Rover down his street and drove toward the entrance to his parking lot. Preoccupied, he glanced out the side window, disgusted at himself, and then back, to find a large dog standing directly in the path of the truck.

Hitting the brakes with both feet, he jerked the steering wheel to the left. The sound of stationary rubber against moving asphalt jarred the air. The old Rover's traction broke loose with a lurch, launching it into a four-wheel slide that drifted, then shuddered to a stop, inches away from a pristine, parked Honda.

Cursing, Mac quickly threw the truck into reverse and backed out of the oncoming lane and climbed out. Walking around to the front, he found the street empty except for random piles of wind-swept leaves. Muttering, he got back into the truck and was barely rolling when he slammed on the brakes again, the Rover stalling in response.

A dog. A dog as big as a wolf. A dog that would leave teeth marks on a man's body similar to those of a wolf. And the imprints would be almost indistinguishable if the dog was a wolf hybrid!

Chapter 11

With squealing tires, Mac whipped the Rover around and headed back to the zoo, pushing the old rig as fast as it would go. If he was lucky, there would still be prints of a dog at the wolf enclosure. Paw prints that looked like a wolf's, but not quite—and more important, they'd be *outside* the enclosure.

Decker would have come in through Hargreve's gate and waited until Jeff and Watermann were at the other end of the grounds. No one would have heard Stewart's yells for help. Mac ran the possible scenario over and over in his mind on the way. But each time he smacked up against Decker's solid alibi.

Decker had been playing poker with a roomful of guards at O'Malley's house the night Stewart died. He had stepped out to get more money, but only briefly, and he had a bank slip with the date and time to prove it.

Decker couldn't have killed Stewart and been at the bank at the same time. He would have needed at least an hour or more to do both. Enough time that his lengthy absence would have been noticed, especially by men in the security business.

Mac flung the Rover to the side of the road and screeched to a halt beside a pay telephone booth. Leaping out, he sorted through his pocket change, found a quarter, and dialed the security chief. O'Malley's wife got him to the phone.

"Chief, sorry to bother you, but I have to ask you another question about the night that Donald Stewart died."

"Sure, Mac, what's up?"

"You left the poker game when Jeff Vincent called that night around nine-thirty or so. Did anybody else leave the game a little earlier?"

"Let's see. Decker went out to get some money but came right back. Some of the fellas left later, around midnight. The rest were still here when I got back. Why?"

"Still trying to sort things out. How long was Decker gone?"

"Half an hour. Maybe a tick more. He was out only two hands, maybe three, then played till about two in the morning."

Discouraged, Mac leaned back against the smooth glass of the phone booth. There was no way Decker could have gotten from O'Malley's house to the bank, to the zoo, killed Stewart, and back to the poker game in less than an hour. The zoo business alone, at professional speed, would have taken almost that amount of time. Another lousy idea.

"Thanks, Chief, that's what I thought." Mac hung up and stood staring out through the glass, trying to make the pieces fit. No matter how he turned them, forced them, pounded on them, they wouldn't go. Decker couldn't have been two places at once.

Mac opened the booth's door and leaned against the metal frame, letting the night air cool him down. He watched absentmindedly as a young woman drove up to an automatic bank machine across the street, got out, and punched in her secret code. After a few seconds the machine responded. She opened the small metal compartment, removed her money and her receipt, and waited for her card, shifting impatiently from foot to foot. Glancing down at the receipt, she shrugged, dropped it into a small, black trash can at her feet, pocketed the cash, and hurried back to her compact car. She drove off, a flush and happy woman.

Modern technology is truly wonderful, Mac thought. Like magic you put in a worthless piece of plastic and get back legal tender and a paper testimony to just how badly you've managed it all.

Some people can't stand to know just how close to the red line they really are, so they don't look at the tattletale receipt the machine faithfully spits out. They just drop it like something diseased into the small, black trash cans at their feet—an electric hand of excitement grabbed Mac just above the Adam's apple—a trash can that wouldn't be emptied until the next morning. Plenty of time to let a customer repent and retrieve it or let a murderer select one for the right time and place and walk merrily away with an alibi.

A grumpy pigeon roosting on top of the phone booth opened one disdainful eye as the big man ran whooping across the street to the bank trash can.

•   •   •

Jeff Vincent came out of the security booth as the Rover edged onto the zoo's grounds. Mac could see Nat Watermann moving around inside the small building.

"Hey, Doc, you want me to get your cat?"

"No, that's okay, I need to get something from my desk. I can pick him up on the way out. Mind if I park this heap by my office? I shouldn't be too long."

"I'm not supposed to let vehicles in at night, but, well, guess I owe you one. I'm startin' my rounds again and'll be back in an hour or so. Page me if you want out sooner." Jeff swung the gate open and waved Mac through.

Mac parked the car out of sight inside the pachyderms' lower-level ramp, just in case someone came onto the grounds. The fewer people who knew he was there, the better.

Leaving his treatment bag on the passenger seat, Mac entered the cat compound and walked down the side hallway, then unlocked his office door and went in, leaving the door ajar. The phone rang as if on cue.

"Hello?"

"MacIntire, I've been looking all over for you. Beginning to think you skipped."

"What and miss your sunny disposition? Listen, Kirby, I got something hot. I can prove beyond a doubt that Stewart wasn't killed by the wolves, and I can make a damn good case as to who did.

"You remember Stewart's left arm? It was pretty torn up but there was one perfect set of imprints of upper teeth. Good enough that your lab could take a casting. *That* will prove the wolves didn't do it."

"Then who did?"

"A dog."

"Excuse me?"

"In the wild the need to hunt creates a skull and snout that's long and narrow, with teeth that are large and well spaced. In the domesticated dog, who doesn't spend its life killing prey, the muzzle has become shortened and the teeth more crowded. If we take a cast of the teeth marks on Stewart's arm and compare the ratio between the width of the roof of the animal's mouth and the length of its upper row of teeth, I'll stack my career on it, we'll find they came from a domestic dog, not a wolf.

"It's the only way to completely rule out the wolves. A blood typing can't clear them, since the wolf and the dog are serologically related. They both have a diploid chromosome number of seventy-eight—"

"Hey, Doc, you're losing me."

"Sorry, what I mean is, we've already determined that the blood found on Toka was not human. That was easy. An animal's blood has more antigens on it than a man's. The test did tell us that the blood wasn't Stewart's. And it told us that the blood came from a canine—but that could be either a wolf or a dog. They have the same ancestors.

"We assumed it was Toka's blood because we weren't looking for a dog. Or any other animal, for that matter. After all, who'd expect to find some *other* animal inside a wolf enclosure? At least, one large enough to kill a man.

"The only way to determine exactly what attacked Stewart is by the dental formation. And, if I'm right, I should also find paw prints—which I'm here looking for—somewhere outside the enclosure."

"You mean to tell me that a bunch of teeth marks on the victim's arm can tell us if the attack was made by a dog or a wolf?" Kirby asked.

"Exactly. Stewart was worried that over the generations the zoo confinement altered the structure of wolves' heads. The longer they're confined, the more domestic-like wolves become. They lose their social structure, their hunting ability, even the length of their legs shortens.

"But Toka and most of his adult pack were wild born, so their heads and teeth formation are true wolf. Stewart had started a catalog of plaster molds from them. We can compare his molds against a casting taken from Stewart's arm. And then, if that's right, I also know who killed Stewart."

"The guy with the mamba."

Mac's jaw dropped. "How . . . ?"

"The FBI just got back on that Ralph Danesto. Seems he's a third-world mercenary who's been enjoying a little vacation with us. Ralph Danesto is an alias for William Decker."

A soft footstep directly behind Mac preceded the chill of blunt metal pressed up against his lower jaw. A diamond glittered on a large hand wrapped lightly around the checkered walnut grip of a Browning Hi-Power automatic.

"MacIntire? You there?" Kirby asked.

The gun waved toward the phone.

"That's very interesting. Nice work. Keep me posted." Mac slowly replaced the receiver as a second hand tightened on the back of his shirt collar.

"Glad you could make the party, Doc. We've been waiting for you," Decker said. "Could say you're the main attraction."

The gun barrel nestled almost lovingly down into the soft depression just below Mac's right earlobe. He walked forward obediently, imagining how it would feel as the bullet exited through his forehead.

Decker herded him down the long hallway into the cat treatment area, the New Balance sneakers squeaking on the linoleum floor. A single overhead light bulb turned the room into a stark-yellow square edged by murky corners. The cat enclosure's gate stood wide open.

Stretched out in the middle of the area was a tiger, twelve feet from nose to tail, the unmistakable Duke. Mac could see the rise and fall of the big cat's chest. One huge five-inch paw twitched occasionally. The cat had been tranquilized and Mac knew immediately what Decker had in mind.

Mac slowly turned to face him. The light bulb cast dark shadows down onto Decker, his eye sockets receding, the face a skin-wrapped skull. He motioned Mac closer to the sleeping cat and then took half a dozen steps backward toward Mac's black treatment bag on the floor. Decker held the cold-blue steel 9-mm pistol in a rock-steady hand. His expression was strangely indifferent but his eyes glittered darkly. The same eyes as the mamba's. Decker was a man who killed like most people have breakfast. Nothing exciting, just the usual everyday fare of high-fiber cereal.

"You shoulda stayed out of it, Doc. I tried to warn you. Would have helped your longevity."

"Guess I'm slow on the uptake."

Decker reached down into Mac's treatment bag, lying at his feet, and pulled out the blowgun. There wasn't any question that it contained M5050, the tranquilizer's reversing drug.

"Wait a minute, Decker. At least tell me why you killed Stewart."

Decker grinned, with a slow, self-satisfied motion. "And Joanne. And Hargreve. And Cristos. Don't underestimate me, I'm good at this."

"Never crossed my mind."

"Hargreve and Cristos tried to set me up. They hired me, indirectly, through Cristos's family, who give me these kind of jobs from time to time. A little pocket money, you know? Anyway, my job was to make H. L.'s death look like an accident. Poaching can be real convenient.

"I was just finishing up when another hit man arrived, with my name on the contract. Those bastards, Hargreve and Cristos, tried to welch out. The hit was supposed to take care of me and then send H. L.'s ring as a signal that it was over. But I got him instead, sent the ring, and came home, the dutiful zookeeper."

"But Hargreve and Cristos must have known something was wrong when you showed up," Mac said, stalling.

"They didn't know I was H. L.'s gun. All they had was a name, Danesto. My other identity. But Cristos eventually figured it out—through my connection with his family—so we cut a deal. Minus Hargreve. I was to take care of the finer details, ya might say, in exchange for a major cut of Hargreve's share."

"You and Cristos double-crossed Hargreve. . . . Nice touch, Decker, double-crossing a double-crosser. But why kill Joanne? She had nothing to do with it."

"She knew the ring hadn't been returned with H. L.'s body—she was at the reading of the will—and figured out that in order for Ed Hargreve to have it he had to be connected to his father's death. I killed her to keep her quiet, and to add a little leverage to my position with the Bobsey Boys. Joanne was just a finer detail.''

Decker's laugh was a flat, heart-stopping sound. Mac felt prickles of fear seep in around the edges, making the back of his neck tingle. Right at the very nape of his hair. Right where Duke would sink in two inches of teeth.

"But these guys tried to knock you off. Why take the chance of coming back?" Mac asked.

"Blackmail. Cristos and Hargreve didn't know who I was. Hargreve had his father killed for the fifty-five-million estate and I figured part of that—the lion's share—was mine. Sort of their penance for betrayal.''

"You were expecting honor among thieves? But how did Stewart figure in?"

"Stewart had that PI sniffing around. He got a lead on Hargreve's problem with that New Jersey embezzlement, which told him what was going on here. Which led to Cristos and his family. And *they* are my employers. That didn't exactly leave me a lot of choice.''

"So you killed Rorke, too," Mac said softly.

"I can't take full credit. Cristos called his family back home to take care of Rorke and ship him up to you. Thought it might get you to back off. Guess I read you wrong, MacIntire.'' Decker took a step to the side, lining himself up for a better shot. "Those two had it really sewn up, as director and financial officer. And, man, Cristos could sure do some sweet book work. A real talent, he had.''

"Had?"

Decker laughed the dead sound. Mac felt his stomach go queasy. He knew where the funnel-web spiders had come from and who had introduced him to the elephants.

"Kinda figured Cristos would try something fancy, though. He told me the embezzlement system was all in place and he was skimming off the mother lode, so we didn't need Hargreve anymore. Cristos would stay on as chief financial officer, no matter. And Hargreve was gettin' real twitchy.

"I shot him that night in his office, and then found papers in the safe showing Cristos had transferred a ton of money into an outside bank account in his name. That told me what Cristos was up to. Had to chase him all the way to the airport." Decker's lips pulled back savagely. "But he was more than happy to tell me all about the account. Now I'm richer 'n God."

"And Stewart's murder? Just another detail?" Mac asked.

Decker shrugged.

"How'd you make his murder look like Toka did it?"

The mercenary beamed, pleased with his creativity. "My good buddy, Satan. Brought him in through Hargreve's private entrance while Stewart was in the wolf enclosure. Dropped the dividing gate to block off the pack and took Satan in." Decker's eyes sparkled in the dim light. "Damnedest thing I ever saw, though. That sucker, Toka, came right over the fence—to protect Stewart. Course it was too late. Satan's as good at what he does as I am. Never seen a wolf defend a man before, though. Took Satan on full time. Thought for sure somebody'd hear 'em." Decker shook his head. "Real shame I couldn't let 'em finish it. Would have been interesting to see which one won. Satan was bleedin' like a faucet by the time I got him out of there. Then I raised the dividing gate back up and left."

"Why didn't you just shoot Toka?" Mac asked.

"Professional courtesy." Decker grinned widely, showing teeth.

Mac stared at him. Shed the clothes and Decker was as much of a predator as any wild animal. And it was all the more heinous that the motive was nothing but calculated, self-serving greed. Wild animals kill for their survival; man kills for more personal reasons.

The mercenary backed away slowly. Putting the automatic into his pocket, he raised the blowgun to his lips and fired a cartridge into the cat's flank. Right on target. Within seconds the tiger began to stir.

"Had a little practice with these myself while doing a job in South America. Always liked 'em. Nice and quiet. And don't set off any airport alarms. Well, thanks, Doc," he said. "Nothin' personal, you understand."

"Of course."

Stepping outside through the exit door, Decker padlocked it behind him. Mac watched as Duke struggled unsteadily to his feet. Mac figured he had two, maybe three, minutes to get out of the pen before dinner was served.

Chapter 12

Mac shrank back involuntarily as the tiger staggered past him. Still disoriented, Duke didn't realize he had company inside the enclosure. Massive paws made soft treading noises on the hard cement floor as Duke struggled to shake off the drug. Groggy twin gold eyes glared in Mac's direction. The tiger wandered aimlessly by, just beyond arm's length. Mac quickly scanned the enclosure for a means of escape.

The pen was secured on one side by heavy chain-link fencing and a now-padlocked door. Two walls of solid cement soared uninterrupted to the twenty-foot-high ceiling. The fourth wall contained the cat's entryway into the public's glass viewing area. Mac edged in that direction.

The viewing room had one glass wall across its face; the back and side walls enclosed a naturalistic setting of boulders and massive logs displayed against a painted mural. The cats climbed the floor-to-ceiling log structures with ease, like children on a jungle gym.

On one side wall, three feet from the ceiling and hidden from the public's view, was a rarely used mesh grate door that allowed the keepers access to the top of the exhibit. Stewart had been insistent that Mac memorize every gate and door at the zoo.

Stewart had said it might one day save his life. Mac mouthed a silent thank-you to his friend.

Getting up to that grate was his only chance. Duke would shake off the effects of the drug in moments and be ready for a man-sized game of cat and mouse.

Mac inched past the still-confused cat, who blearily shook his giant head. Stepping toward the entryway, Mac could feel the cat's hot breath as he panted open mouthed. Even in his drugged state Duke instinctively tracked Mac's movements. One lip curled up, a low rumble rattled the air.

Reaching the foot of the biggest log, Mac took hold of the trunk, placed his boot on the bark, and cautiously climbed upward, one eye on the tiger. The log seemed to stretch up forever toward the twenty-foot summit.

At the point where the log reached the ceiling, and across a six-foot span of open air, was a narrow ledge just beneath the grate door. The ledge was designed to prevent a 600-pound cat from reaching it. Or a scared 200-pound man, Mac thought. His only chance was to reach that ledge.

His work boots slipping on the claw-scarred wood, Mac muscled his way upward. Each step brought a small gain in progress. He dug his foot in hard. A large piece of bark broke loose and fell, landing just in front of the rapidly recovering cat.

Duke sniffed at the bark, his massive head searching for the source. Mac froze precariously. He dug his fingers into the log, pressed his face down, and tried to control the sound of his strained breathing. His heart's pounding overpowered all his other senses.

The tiger circled the log and raked a lethal set of claws across the bottom. The tranquilizer had not left Duke in one of his better moods.

Mac felt his arms begin to shake and a muscle in his left leg cramp as he supported his full weight. As he shifted slightly to ease the pressure, his boot broke loose from its toehold and he slid downward. Flinging both arms around the log, he slowed his fall to a stop. His breath rushed out in one loud, revealing grunt. The tiger went to full alert, completely conscious, his eyes scanning upward, muscles coiling to attack. Suddenly Duke exploded up the log like a locomotive on a track.

Mac scrambled up onto his knees, forcing his feet under him, clawing his way up the last few feet of log. Reaching the top, he flung himself in a reckless, desperate leap over the yawning gap toward the ledge. He contacted with the wall, his fingers barely hooking the lower edge of the grating, and hung, dangling, twenty feet above concrete.

Duke was at the top of the log in seconds, claws flashing inches away as Mac clung to the door. Dragging himself onto the narrow ledge, Mac recoiled as Duke leaned forward off the log, stretching to capture his prey. The cat's reach reduced the margin of safety to less than three feet. With the tiger this close, there wasn't enough room to lean back and swing open the door. He had to get Duke to back off.

Squeezing a hand through the grating, Mac forced open the slide bolt. He inched over to the far edge of the ledge and pulled on the mesh door. Grabbing the top, he pushed off from the ledge, swinging out at his full length. As the door traveled toward the log, Mac kicked downward with his feet at a point a few feet below the cat. Duke, seeing the movement, whirled toward it, teeth bared, snarls reverberating in the hollow room.

Reaching its farthest position, the door began an excruciatingly slow arc back to the ledge. Mac dragged himself upward hand over hand on the inside of the mesh as it moved. The tiger lunged, one claw snagging Mac's pants leg. Mac kicked frantically, freed his leg, and threw himself through the opening as the door cleared the ledge. Landing heavily on his back on the metal catwalk, he scrambled up, slammed the door shut, and rammed home the bolt. Duke raked empty air, roaring in frustration.

Crouching on the dimly lit walkway, Mac gulped air and tried to think. Decker would return to check on Duke's handiwork. The mercenary was not a man to make the same mistake twice. Mac had to get out of the building.

Sweat stung his eyes as he crept along the catwalk toward the far ladder. His boots echoed loudly on the metal structure. At the bottom of the ladder and five feet to the left was the entrance to the tunnel that connected the compounds. Using the underpass, Mac could get to a phone at the pachyderm entrance ramp or, if he was unusually lucky, to the Rover parked just inside.

He stepped into the tunnel and listened. It was silent and foreboding in the semidarkness. Equipment caught at his feet and cobwebs left silky strands across his face as he felt his way. The zebra skull yawned from the shadows.

Stopping, he held his breath. A rat squeaked as it scrambled over the toe of his boot. He felt his skin crawl, from memories of foreign nights and hungry rodents.

Reaching the pachyderm building, he peered out. The Rover stood waiting, just as he had left it. Mac sprinted over to the cement column in the middle of the room and grabbed for the phone. The receiver cord dangled in his hand, useless, confirming the silence. Mac slowly put it back on the hook. He consciously fought the feeling of panic that threatened to overtake him.

Turning, he ran to the ramp gate. But a new padlock held the iron door securely shut. Mac wiped his dirt-streaked face on the sleeve of his shirt. Time was running out. Decker would be looking for him soon.

He tiptoed to the Rover. If he could ram the gate with the heavy truck he could intercept Jeff and Watermann—if they weren't already dead. Tonight, Decker would leave nothing to chance.

Crawling into the driver's seat, Mac breathed a sigh of relief.

The keys were still in the ignition. Mac turned the key, his hand shaking. Silence. He turned it again. Nothing, not even a click. Leaping out of the truck, he tore open the hood. A severed cable hung from the battery.

Mac walked around to the side of the Rover and sank onto the seat. Kirby was right, he was definitely out of his league. He had to get help. He checked his watch. Even if the guard was still alive, jogging, he wouldn't be in this part of the grounds for another half an hour. Mac had to attract someone's attention. The docent director was the only other person on the grounds. She would be at her post watching the video monitors. Somehow he had to get her attention.

Frantically, Mac scanned the area for something, anything to use. A broken pitchfork, a stack of hay, two coiled garden hoses were all there was. The keepers' lounge, a small adjoining room, held two empty coffee cups, one unemptied ashtray, a few matches, and a used paper napkin. Mac walked back into the ramp area and sat back down in the Rover. He suddenly looked at the truck.

One of Mac's Vietnam buddies, a kid from the inner city, could hot-wire a car in under sixty seconds. Mac knew, he had timed him. It had been quite a tour. Tony had even shown him how to torch the commandant's car one Friday night after a few too many beers.

The pros used a delay system with enough time to get away from the scene. Mac hoped he could remember how to do it. He needed a cigarette and matches.

He crept back to the keepers' lounge and found a half-smoked cigarette and six matches. Returning to the Rover, he unhooked the jerry can from its bracket in the back and poured the gasoline over the dashboard. In the front seat he spread a bale of hay. Lighting the cigarette, Mac stuck it behind the five remaining matches. He prayed five matches would be enough to ignite the fumes. Tony had used a full book.

Mac placed the smoldering bundle up against the front windshield and dumped the remainder of the gasoline onto the hay. He sprinted to the far side of the room and ducked down behind a stack of hay bales. Suddenly Decker appeared at the entrance of the tunnel.

Mac held his breath and prayed for the explosion, his heart pounding. Nothing. He heard footsteps coming toward him.

Decker stepped around the corner of the hay, stopped, and yanked the gun from his belt. As the mercenary turned toward him, Mac lunged, clamping both hands around Decker's wrist. They fell back, wrestling. Decker fought with the ease and agility of a man trained for combat. Mac fought for his life.

A precisely delivered blow to the right temple left Mac dazed. Decker wrenched his arm away, straightened, and aimed the gun. Mac tensed, anticipating the bullet's impact.

An ear-shattering blast suddenly threw both men to the ground; the air was alive with flying glass. The Rover roared into flames.

Momentarily stunned, Mac sat up and looked around. Decker was groggily trying to rise onto one knee, the gun still gripped in his hand. Mac scrambled up, running for the tunnel. He glanced back and saw Decker coming after him.

Mac made it into the darkened tunnel and stumbled, groping, along the wall. He tried to mentally picture where the discarded equipment was as pieces caught at his feet. He ran, unsure, in the half dark. He knew if he fell, he was dead. Decker would use that error.

The rasp of Mac's strained breathing was joined by the hollow sound of lightly running footsteps, coming closer. Mac partially turned, searching for Decker in the dark. Unable to see him, Mac raced forward, the pursuing steps closing, echoing louder, now only yards behind. Mac looked up and saw a rectangle of light at the end of the tunnel. He sprinted for the doorway, unable to think past the yellow glow.

Decker caught up to him as he entered the treatment area. They struggled, battling their way back into the cat's viewing area. Decker fought effortlessly, a fixed smile on his face, pushed close.

A practiced foot behind his heel sent Mac sprawling to the floor. He raised his head and looked up into the diminishing black circle of gun muzzle pointed at his forehead, sited just below the hairline. Mac watched transfixed as the trigger finger moved slowly backward, a fraction of an inch at a time. Decker laughed his flat, dead sound. Mac closed his eyes.

A noise, low and rumbling, came from the right. Mac looked up in time to see a flash of movement, of color, and then a nothing-darkness as his head was slammed back against the concrete.

Coming to a few minutes later, Mac gagged as torrents of water hit him from all directions. Dark figures in the wet mist had hoses trained on Duke, who was dragging Decker by the neck. Watermann yelled to not move.

Mac watched as Decker flailed helplessly against the powerful cat like a skewered insect. Then, with one swift shake of his massive head, Duke stopped the man's thrashing.

Dripping wet, bleeding and bruised, Mac put his head down onto his arms.

Chapter 13

The keepers forced Duke away from Decker's mangled body with the water hose and herded the cat into another enclosure. Kirby ran over to Mac, who sat leaning against the wall, head back, staring at the ceiling.

"You okay, pal?" Kirby asked.

Mac slowly turned his eyes and saw the detective's outstretched hand. Grabbing hold, Kirby swung him to his feet.

"You okay?" Kirby repeated.

"I think I just saw my life in slo-mo," Mac said, water streaming down into his boots. "It needs a little work."

"Whose doesn't."

"Decker had a gun murmuring in my ear when you called. How did you know to come?"

"Knew something wasn't right. You weren't mouthy enough."

The two men headed for the ramp area. "Decker gave me the whole rundown. He was hired to kill H. L. in Africa, but when the deal went sour he came back to blackmail—"

"Ed Hargreve and Alex Cristos," Kirby interrupted.

"How the hell do you know that?"

"A little old lady saw a man slumped over the wheel of a gold Mercedes in the parking lot of Logan Airport this morning and called us. We got there just in time for Cristos to unburden his soul."

"Cristos is dead?"

"As a hammer. Died on the way to the hospital. Decker shot him, and then came back to arrange your aerobics lesson with your furry friend over there," Kirby said.

"Decker said Hargreve and Cristos planned to embezzle the money H. L. left to the zoo. They didn't know who they had hired to kill H. L., but Cristos eventually figured out it was Decker. He and Decker then double-crossed Hargreve. It was Decker I saw Hargreve arguing with and who shot him. Cristos took off in Hargreve's car. Guess he thought he could outfox Decker."

"Then Decker must have killed Rorke?" Kirby asked.

Mac shook his head. "No, Cristos called the Family down in Newark. He didn't want Rorke stumbling across his connections. But Decker did kill Stewart, to turn up the heat on Hargreve and Cristos."

Kirby let out a satisfied sigh and snapped his notebook shut. "I love it when it's neat."

The men walked toward the collection of police uniforms scurrying in and out through the open ramp gate. "So, what's your plans, Doc? Going to stay in the area?"

Mac looked out the door toward the North American compound and its lumps of dark sleeping bison. "Don't know yet. There are a few options I need to explore, someone special I need to talk to."

A slow smile spread across the detective's face. "I bet."

"But the first thing I'm going to do is go tell Toka the good news. Want me to introduce you? He's one great wolf."

"That's your story," Kirby said and yawned, stuffing his notebook into his pocket. He turned on his heel and ambled toward the morgue crew. Deep, hearty laughter floated back.

Mac watched Kirby walk past the still-smoking Rover and, despite himself, began to grin.